A Matter of Honor

A Matter of Honor

LAURA FRANTZ

To all those who delight in books, birds, & blooms

Prologue

London, England
1739

In the glittering, beeswax-scented drawing room of Kensington Palace, Orin Hume stood beside a Palladian window. Clenching his jaw lest he laugh, he and this great cloud of witnesses comprised of the Court watched what resembled a stage play as an especially prominent lady-in-waiting tried to maneuver her wide hoops through a side door. Finally, in a fit of temper, she freed herself, her panniered petticoats shuddering, her lofty wig listing to one side.

The sultry June heat frayed the steadiest nerves and did the heavily made-up courtiers few favors, their lead-painted faces shining, rouged cheeks sliding to chins marked with velvet beauty patches. Did he look equally absurd in their illustrious eyes being clad in plain if finely tailored dark blue? He shunned the requisite high collar in favor of a snow-white stock and wore unadorned silk hose, his only embellishment the diamond-crusted silver buckles on his shoes. His rebelliously unpowdered hair was distinctive and he defied the filthy norm by bathing once a day.

He, a humble Lowland Scots lad, should have been impressed by the flash of jewels and array of silks and laces. But time among the bickering, scheming, flirting Court led to a loathing he found hard to suppress. Despite his rather romantic profession, he had an intensely practical nature and a canny eye for the ridiculous.

"Mr. Hume, I presume?" An elderly matron raised a heart-shaped quizzing glass to look him over. Was she advertising her intentions?

He gave a slight bow, trying to place her.

"Allow me to introduce my niece, Lady Theodosia Spencer."

"Milady," he murmured, meeting the lively eyes of yet another obliging young lass.

"Would you accompany me to the punch bowl, sir?" she asked with a flick of her fan. "And perhaps share a bit of verse?"

"The punch, aye," he said with a smile. "A bit of verse, nay."

She tittered coyly as if he was guilty of flirting with her. "I admit I'm rather excited about the forthcoming royal birthday." Her gaze wandered from him to the canopied throne of the monarch at the far end of the drawing room. "The celebration usually begins in the morning, does it not?"

"With divine service," he said. "Kirk, we Scots call it."

"Followed by your ode in His Majesty's praise as Poet Laureate, set to music by the Master of Music." She accepted the punch he handed her. "And then there's to be an afternoon drawing room and an evening grand ball."

Orin nodded and eyed the courtyard out another window where his sedan chair waited. He always seemed to be standing by palace windows. An escape, he guessed. And escape he did, a quarter of an hour later at midnight. The summer moon hung like a discarded pearl over the palace's once formal gardens which the late Queen Caroline had exchanged for a more natural look. Somewhere near was the royal exotic menagerie, including caged lions and tigers. Many evenings he'd left the palace to the frightful chorus of their roars.

He stood by the Long Water in the moonlit dark, feeling much further than four hundred miles from home. The Queen's Temple crowned the hill above, reminiscent of the old Saxon gatehouse at Wedderburn Castle. How had *The Gentleman's Magazine* described it?

A heap of stones, thrown into a very artful disorder, and curiously embellished with moss and shrubs, to represent rude nature.

Rude nature, aye. That was what he craved after so much civility.

He picked up a stone and skimmed it across the silvery water, the breeze lifting and carrying the scent of the gardens, roses foremost. Apothecary and Maiden's-Blush, Rosamundi and Moss. Even after five years he couldn't distance himself from the scent and the lass who'd become one and the same in his head and heart.

Lady Maryn Lockhart.

1

Edinburgh, Scotland
May, 1740

A wee smirr of rain struck the tenement's windowpanes at twilight, blurring Orin Hume's view of lamplit Edinburgh. Bringing a fist to his mouth, he stifled a yawn, the groan of his grandfather's ancient chair beneath him a reminder of just how long he'd sat stiffly trying to scratch out a few lines on the paper before him.

Poet Laureate of Britain, indeed.

His gaze rose to the room's equally ancient rafters, blackened beams painted with faded unicorns and thistles. Heavy drapes and furnishings carried a distillation of Lowland herbs and Highland spirits. He rarely came here except when he was guest lecturer at the university. He much preferred his London abode, Hume House, at number 70 Dean Street, with its bold red door and overhead fanlight chasing away the shadows. Quiet. Clean. Spare. Not this monstrosity from another century...

If he was inclined to believe in ghosts, this would be the ideal place for his long-departed brother, David Hume, to haunt. "Davie the devil" as some called him had lived here before losing his life to the Jacobite cause in the '15, a lasting lesson on how not to offend the reigning monarch. And now, in an ironic twist, he himself must honor George II's birthday celebration with an ode…or perish. Unless he resigned before the king could axe his position.

Inking his quill again, he dashed out a few haphazard lines, hearing Mrs. Archer softly singing a hymn as she approached with what surely was a toddy. A timid knock and then—

"Master Orin? Surely this dreich night calls for a bit o' cheer."

He let go his quill and stood to greet Hume's Land's house-keeper, steam rising from the tray that shook in her gnarled hands. She set it, or rather plopped it, atop the table near the hearth and he thanked her. She and the butler, Simms, were so old and had served the Humes so long they seemed as much a part of the house as the smoky timbers and drafty windows. And she had an uncanny knack of sensing his unspoken thoughts, probably since she'd known him since he was a wee lad.

"Simms told me ye're going to the theater tonight." She tarried in the doorway. "Have ye finished lecturing at the college?"

"As of today, aye. Now I must—um, puzzle out some poetry for His Majesty's Birthnight Ball for later this year and finish two plays I've committed to for Drury Lane and Covent Garden."

"I thought I heard the laird mention yer return to Wedderburn Castle for Lady Charis's summer debut when he was last here."

"Och, I canna forget that." But he had, nearly. He moved toward the fragrant toddy, stepping into the warmth emanating from the hearth fire. "Where is that letter?"

"I believe Simms put it in the cupboard." She smiled as if to encourage him. "I do hope ye go. 'Tis been an age since ye've been home."

An age. She was being kind. "Thank you, Mrs. Archer—for the toddy and the reminder of my Lowland obligations."

The door clicked closed and he sank into another chair, the worn seat nearly sagging to the thin carpet. The toddy was not the comfort he needed as he fixed his gaze on the cupboard that held the letter on the far wall, oft used to store items of importance. What had Charis written?

In seconds he'd retrieved it, the foolscap elegantly decorated with his niece's signature fairies and sprigs of heather, a habit since childhood that belied her eighteen years. Moving a candle closer, he studied the invitation.

Dear Uncle Orin,

Lest you forget your favorite niece ...

He smiled. His *only* niece.

... the youngest child of your brother, Everard, and dear sister-in-law, Blythe, I am here to remind—nay, beg—you to return to Wedderburn Castle and escort me for a round of balls and entertainments beginning in June.

The honor is all mine, of course. I've adored you since birth and am in awe of your prodigious talents of the pen. No one else can boast arriving on the arm of the country's noted Poet Laureate.

Please come home and put the tragic circumstance of the past behind you. 'Tis best accepted if not forgotten. Carpe diem, my Latin tutor used to tell me. There's no one I'd rather seize the day with than you.

Devotedly,
Charis

Setting the letter aside, he downed the toddy in another throat-searing gulp.

Tragic circumstance, aye.

Accepted, nay.

2

$\mathcal{M}$aryn Lockhart traded Thistle Cottage for the rear garden held between high stone walls, the gamekeeper's Border Collie, Bassett, on her heels. Dew filigreed every fern and flower. May's bright scent was everywhere, the sun buttering the surrounding stones with warm light.

Here she wasn't Lady Maryn any longer, just Maryn. Five years she'd shut herself away since the ordeal that sent her reeling. Only she hadn't healed, just hidden, her visible wounds turned to scars. On her best days she rarely thought of the tragedy. On her worst days it was all she thought about. Here in the Lowlands near the North Sea, few had pity on her or stared. Few knew she was even at Thistle Cottage.

She had Grandfather Lockhart to thank for that. He alone had seen her struggle and settled her far from society. When she'd first set eyes on this charming cottage on Lockhart land, it had left her smitten. With its rustic thatched roof, stone and timber construction, and leaded windows, it was so smothered in ivy and roses it seemed more fairytale. Her favorite feature was the carving over the lintel noting the date of its construction. 1585. Old things had always delighted her heart.

Safely nestled within the shadow of the gamekeeper's lodge, Maryn felt she had a guard at her disposal. Mr. Leslie lived there with his ageing wife, who was almost as much a recluse as she.

Gates to Lockhart Hall, numerous *no trespassing* signs, and deep ditches kept any visitors at bay. When Grandfather Lockhart was in residence and away from Edinburgh, he rarely entertained family and friends. He only desired her company.

"I wish you would come to the Hall, my dear," became his gentle refrain.

"If you were to stop visiting me at the cottage I might," she said with a smile.

Had it been last Hogmanay since she'd seen him? How she'd once loved the Twelve Days of Christmas before the shadow cast by the accident eclipsed the joys of the season. Today the woes of winter seemed distant. She stepped into a beam of sunlight and stood, eyes closed, as light chased away the darkness. For a few seconds she yielded to the dazzling warmth before continuing on, a basket on her good arm.

The snowdrops of Candlemas and jonquils of early spring had given way to purple plumes of allium. In the language of flowers, allium signified patience of which she had little. She chafed again at the mail's delay, dwelling instead on the camellias that soon filled her basket in a rosy profusion of pinks, compliments of the East India Company who'd brought them to Britain.

She grew a great deal from seed and under glass, sometimes taking cuttings from Lockhart Hall's extensive gardens. Grandfather had built her what he called the tiniest orangery in all Scotland, an extension of Thistle Cottage and heated by charcoal braziers. It even boasted a fruited pineapple within its glass walls.

Beyond the enclosed garden were glades of bluebells interspersed with meadowsweet and wild thyme and Lady's-mantle. She often ventured out on foot at twilight, having given up riding. Fear kept her from horses, or even carriages if she could help it—especially a sleigh—though the music of sleigh bells carried far on a hushed winter's day.

Since this was the Sabbath she was mindful that her maidservant, Rosemary, spent the day with her family in the near village of Ladykirk. A chatterbox by nature, her absence lent a profound quiet to the holy day, and left Maryn missing kirk. How long had it been since she'd darkened the door of the old stone building on the banks of the River Tweed?

Sitting down on a stone bench, she set her blooming basket aside. Of all the thorns in her life, missing kirk was the sharpest. What did the Almighty think of her self-imposed exile? She still wrestled with uncertainty, especially crushing on the Sabbath. Rather than soothe her, the peace and beauty of the blooming garden seemed to magnify her solitary state. She longed to share such loveliness with someone but only the Collie pressed against her petticoats and looked up at her adoringly. Bassett would have to do.

"G'morn, m'lady. Some fresh eggs for ye." The voice spilling over the garden wall was reassuringly familiar. "Feels like rain, does it nae?"

"Indeed it does, Mrs. Leslie." At her feet grew deep blue blossoms, their black button centers tightly furled and foretelling a change of weather. "The anemones agree with you."

"Have ye any needs before I hie to market tomorrow?"

"I've need of ink and pounce primarily but you already ken that, thank you."

A chuckle. "Ye're a lady of letters, truly. Anything for the post?"

"I'm still awaiting word of—something." Maryn's voice faded then rebounded. "Thank you for the eggs. I've in mind a fluffy, buttery omelette."

"Och! Ye're a fine cook, too, with Rosemary away. A blessed Sabbath to ye, m'lady."

A fluffy, buttery omelette for dinner and leftover salmon for supper brought the Sabbath to a close. Maryn stirred the fire's embers and added more coal before heating the kettle for tea. Night crept in like Jamesina, the cat, while Bassett lay outside the half open door. Waiting for the kettle to sing, Maryn sat down at her writing desk and moved a lit candle closer. Opening the drawer, she ignored the breathless tightening in her chest and took out a few bank notes. Precious few.

Thus far her literary endeavors had enabled her to become a woman of independent means, even a benefactress, since leaving home. Payment for her plays wasn't always timely despite the astonishing run of *Parsons and Petticoats*. But the curtain had come down on that performance. One couldn't live long on one's literary successes.

She'd further depleted her funds with her support of London's Foundling Hospital. The plight of abandoned children continually moved her. But she would not—could not—borrow from Grandfather though he was always there to supply her with whatever she asked for should she ask. She was simply loathe to ask.

Her gaze rose to the window as if a post rider would materialize before her eyes.

Where *was* the mail?

3

Orin opened a side door of the Theatre Royal, surprised to find it unlocked after a late performance the previous night. Stage manager, Ross Castle, stood in the hall speaking with the darling of Edinburgh's audiences. Ella Claire smiled as he approached.

"Ah, Mr. Hume, you've sufficiently recovered from last night's play, I hope?"

"Given all I had to do was occupy a velvet-lined box, the question needs redirecting." He smiled down at her, struck by how petite she was. Beneath the lights her presence seemed larger than life. "Though I did enjoy the exertion of tossing flowers on stage after your performance."

She gave a little laugh. "Far better than orange rinds and rotten eggs." Pushing aside the fabric of her cape, she revealed one fading blossom pinned to her bodice. "Now I must bid both of you gentlemen adieu so I can retire and have my pre-performance rest."

She spun away with a last lingering look, leaving Orin to wonder just where in Auld Reekie she lived. Not too far from the theater, he guessed.

He turned back to a yawning Castle. "So comedies of manners are finally alive and well in Edinburgh."

Castle's chuckle was gleeful as he quoted a well-known verse. *"In every distant clime Great Britain knows, The Thistle springs promiscuous with the Rose, While in all points with other lands she vied, The stage alone to Scotland was denied."*

"Scotland is decades behind England's thespians. But in truth I've not ever been so entertained by London's theater as I was here last night. It makes me reconsider my return there."

"Miss Claire is a consummate professional, you mean."

"Aye, but there's a genius of a playwright at its core."

Castle pushed open the door of his office. "'Tis best discussed over a dram."

The shadowed interior bore heavily draped windows and an unlit chandelier. Playbills and handbills, even banknotes, littered a desk. Castle motioned toward a sofa and chairs framing a fireplace. A gilded painting of Shakespeare himself presided over the mantel.

"All I can say is that we performed *Parsons and Petticoats* thirty-two nights to a packed house who's grown tired of the old Bard, at least for the time being."

"Mayhap after the long winter we've had a little levity is called for." Orin hadn't laughed so hard in months, mayhap years. Therapeutic, that. "Who is this mysterious playwright?"

Castle handed him the whisky. "You've been following *Tatler*."

"It is the leading literary journal—and the most reliable." Orin sat, booted feet to the fire. "There's something oddly familiar about the work. A recognizable rhythm to the words. The wit."

He felt a flicker of nostalgia that swept him back to the lad he'd once been—and a lass who never seemed to escape his thoughts. Might the playwright be...Maryn? The performance had the unmistakable ring of her about it. *Utter nonsense.*

Common sense shot down the wistful notion. Would he never forget her?

Castle shrugged. "Few shun such acclaim, though this thespian wishes to remain anonymous and works through a contact here in Edinburgh."

"Intriguing, even admirable," Orin murmured as the burn of whisky cleared his throat.

"Some might choose to remain hidden given the slightly scandalous name of the play. *Parsons and Petticoats* alone is enough to keep many at bay."

Orin shrugged. "But the production is remarkably chaste. Nary a tawdry line or innuendo, just pure mirth. That's part of its genius."

Castle's gaze was shrewd. "You'd like to make the playwright's acquaintance, I'd wager."

"I'd like to extend my admiration, my thanks for an evening well spent."

"If I learn more I'll send word." Castle set down his empty glass. "What I can tell you is another play is promised from this anonymous thespian, this time a farce."

"A farce in the spirit of George Farquhar or Susanna Centlivre?"

"Not if the literary critics have anything to do with it. Alexander Pope, especially."

Orin held back an expletive. "Pope is a vicious critic of all but his own work."

Castle chuckled wryly. "They're all hostile to newcomers who steal their thunder."

"In this case they have reason to be."

Pondering it, Orin took note of the time. Bidding Castle farewell, he left the theater to focus on his real reason for tarrying in Edinburgh. Relying on a sedan chair, he hied to the east end of the Luckenbooths and the sign of Mercury with winged heels that marked Allen Ramsay's popular bookshop. A biblio-phile's paradise, Ramsay loaned books to patrons in a circulating library that Orin wanted to emulate. Here the leading literary lights and wits of the city gathered and he felt at home.

Stepping into the large shop that smelled of leather and paper, coffee and ink, Orin nearly sighed with pleasure. His vision for the future had shifted and sharpened as Ramsay encouraged him to further enlighten the Lowlands, the largely illiterate place of his birth.

But what would that entail? And could sharing his passion for literature be done?

The next morning, Orin took the Great North Road from Edinburgh to the Lowlands. With highwaymen thick as fleas for hundreds of miles, he was glad Lord Lovell rode alongside him. Tall and spare, Lovell, an Englishman, also bore a dirk and pistols beneath his cape. The lengthy journey to Wedderburn Castle gave them both ample time to consider the coming social season.

Friends since their university days in Edinburgh, Lovell had met and formed a tentative attachment to Orin's niece, Lady Charis Hume. But circumstances and distance had wedged themselves between them and they'd lost touch. When he'd learned she was to have a social season, he decided to join Orin at her debut. A surprise if you will.

"I only hope she remembers me fondly," Lovell mused. "I recall our last meeting like yesterday. She performed during a musical evening, and I accompanied her on the violin. Does she still play the harp?"

"I can't say. It's been some time since I've been home."

"I confess my trepidation at seeing her again is only rivaled by my meeting her father, Lord Wedderburn."

Orin checked a knowing smile. "My eldest brother is somewhat intimidating."

"Everard Hume is certainly that. He and the countess have five sons if I remember rightly. I've nearly lost count of your expanding family as they rival a large herd of Lowland sheep."

With a chuckle, Orin didn't refute him. "None of the sons are home at present which makes it somewhat easier for you and is probably why the task of squiring Charis for the season falls to me."

"Best name them anyway lest I commit some unforgettable error."

"Starting from oldest to youngest, there's Alexander, the laird's heir, currently in the American colonies on business. Then there's Alisdair and Marcel and Leander, together on the continent enjoying a Grand Tour. The youngest, Roland, is in Glasgow at university."

"Will the laird object to an Englishman courting his only daughter?"

"Not when he wed a Northumberland lass years ago. Nor," Orin replied tongue-in-cheek, "will he hold it against you that you're heir to a duchy. Besides, courting is not matrimony."

"I suppose Lady Charis has a bevy of suitors." Lovell looked perplexed. "How much society do you think I'll have to endure to pursue her?"

Endure was the right word, at least where London was concerned. "Scottish society is a bit more lax. None of that foolish Court protocol where we're headed."

"Since I'm a sassenach as Highlanders say, I'm at a decided disadvantage. Suppose she'd rather have a Scot?"

Would she? Personally, Orin had never considered marrying anyone outside Scotland's borders himself though that romantic deed was far from done. "She used to ask about you in her letters, though to be honest she didn't mention you last time."

"I've lost my edge then." Lovell sent Orin a sharp look. "Enough about me. Why has no English lass turned your head? You've been in London for years, ever since the—"

The unfinished sentence held the lash of a whip. "Ever since the accident, aye." Orin gestured to a galleried coaching inn at a crossroads. He'd rather talk of anything but the accident. "Let's stop here. The *Red Lion* is newer and less vermin-ridden than the rest."

Halfway to Wedderburn Castle.

Orin had an odd, swelling suspicion this homecoming might be of far more significance to himself than Lord Lovell.

4

The Monday following the Sabbath, Maryn heard Rosemary humming a hymn long before she appeared at the cottage door. In one hand the smiling maid clutched a book, the other a basket.

"Forgive me, Lady Maryn. Mam needed me longer this morn and said to thank ye for the book o' verse." She returned it to the parlor shelf with brisk efficiency. "She's sent freshly made bannocks and some asparagus from our garden. I'll stir up that maltaise sauce with a lemon and orange ye're so fond of for supper if ye like."

"Bethankit," Maryn said. "You're welcome to take more time at home if needs be. A close-knit family is one of life's best gifts."

"Truly, milady." Rosemary's usual exuberance dimmed briefly. "I've also brought a wee bit o' blather from around Berwickshire."

"Oh?" Maryn brightened. Rosemary's news added color to her days. "I'm a captive audience then."

As the maid went about the cottage tidying this or that, she shared her gleanings. "Reverend Percival's wife has pleurisy and was missing from service yesterday but Ladykirk's circular stair tower is finally complete. A bonny sight!"

Maryn tried to imagine it finished. Built in the sixteenth century, the old kirk seemed in need of constant mending.

"A vile fever's kept a few parishioners at home and Dr. Sinclair quite busy. Little Tommy Forsyth fell from an apple tree and hurt his pate but is better. Four new bairns have been born in the parish lately, all thriving."

"Praise be," Maryn said, wishing she could call on them in person rather than send gifts in the name of Grandfather and Lockhart Hall. She'd known these tenant families since birth, most of them. Once she'd attended their christenings with her mother.

Rosemary went into the kitchen. "As for gentry such as yerself, the social season shall open with a ball at Wedderburn Castle a fortnight hence."

"Lady Charis's debut, I suppose." Maryn smoothed her voice to hide the beat of hurt beneath. How long had it been since she'd seen the Humes?

"She's quite bonny, I hear, and verra like her mother the countess."

Lady Wedderburn was nearly a saint in these parts. And Maryn hadn't forgotten the kind notes she'd sent to Lockhart Hall after the accident. Suddenly Wedderburn Castle seemed far closer than the eight miles betwixt them.

Rosemary began trimming the asparagus, her voice carrying from the kitchen. "'Tis said one of her uncles will squire her for the season."

Though he went unnamed, Maryn suspected the very one. Unwillingly, she took stock of the Humes in the sudden silence. Everard, the laird, was alive and well. The family's black sheep, David, had died fighting for the Jacobites in the last Rising. Ronan and Bernard Hume had wed and were living with their wives and children on Berwickshire estates. The twins, Alistair and Malcolm, resided in Glasgow as doctor and barrister.

And the youngest? She knew far too well his whereabouts and happenings. Her gaze landed on the stack of literary magazines in a corner. *Tatler* tracked Orin Hume's every move.

"I'm sure Lady Charis will make a brilliant match." With that terse summation, Maryn went to her writing desk and took out a fresh sheet of foolscap, wanting to quell her sudden disquiet.

Nothing settled her quite like writing. Who was it that said the pen tames the most formidable beast? She'd always prefer her comedies of manners to real life, the people on the page to those in person. Lady Cowslip and Lord Folderol, Captain Quicksand and Parson Aflutter made amusing companions. Thankfully, these fictitious friends never failed to help her forget the past and the real personages that peopled it.

After supper, Maryn and Bassett went for a walk as the sun sank in soft spring splendor. Though Thistle Cottage was surrounded by sheltering trees on a hill, if one ventured further the whole world seemed to fall away. Maryn could see for miles across heather-clad hills rife with castle ruins and a distant village or two. Rosemary was a mere speck on the path that led to her family's humble home a mile away.

She'd stood here in many a changing season weighing the merits of each. Autumn often wrapped the landscape in a gauzy haar scarf, winter a snowy white fur, and summer a riot of silken colors. Spring tiptoed in, green and damp and misty though tonight it seemed almost summery. The sudden dust storm on the main road in the distance certainly bespoke a dry spell.

Conscious her rose-hued gown might stand out on the hill, Maryn lowered herself to the grass as Bassett continued on in pursuit of a butterfly. Her attention narrowed to the distant horses. Two riders. At a canter. They left the main road and veered toward Wedderburn Castle's main gate. Nothing odd about that. People were always going to and from the Hume's ancestral seat. She relaxed somewhat. Even if the riders had spied the lass on the far hill they'd merely think her a tenant on Lockhart lands.

Hardly the granddaughter of a duke.

5

When the dust of the ride cleared, Wedderburn Castle rose up in all its weathered grandeur, a great pile of stone enhanced with an astonishing number of Palladian windows. Home to the Humes since the fifteenth century, it had undergone numerous improvements since the current laird married his English bride.

Dismounting in the stable yard, Orin and Lord Lovell stood on centuries-old cobbles and took in a well and mews. A groom led their mounts away as the two men started for the castle, leather portmanteaus in hand.

"Do they know I'm coming?" Lovell asked with sudden concern, falling into step beside him.

"I didna ken you were coming till we encountered each other in Edinburgh lately." Orin still thought it a master stroke of luck. Or Providence? "I could have sent word ahead, but sometimes 'tis better to ask forgiveness than permission."

"Blast, Hume!" Lovell's answering smile was wry. "You are no help for my courting nerves."

"Lady Charis likes surprises, so that is in your favor."

"Glad I am of that." Lovell removed his cocked hat. "And Lady Wedderburn is very hospitable if I remember correctly."

"As hospitable as Lord Wedderburn is stern, aye."

They passed through the rear entrance that brought them to a marble-floored hall in back of the castle's central staircase.

Servants went about their duties with downcast eyes and quiet feet though the head housekeeper welcomed them warmly.

"Master Orin," Mrs. Candlish said fondly, using the address of his boyhood. "An unexpected pleasure. Shall I have a room readied for your guest?"

Introductions made and details arranged, Lovell followed the housekeeper upstairs while Orin sought the drawing room most used by family. Meandering down corridors brought him face to face with closed double doors. He paused to brush the dust from his garments and straighten his stock, slightly ill at ease. How had three months lengthened to three years? At least his family had come to see him at Hume House in London or else he would have missed them altogether.

After a slight knock, he pushed the mahogany doors open. On the other side was Lady Charis staring back at him as if she'd seen a ghost. For a moment they faced off, speechless.

"Uncle?" Leaving a windowseat where she'd been reading, Charis flew around the furniture to meet him. Tall and lithe, she closed the distance and nearly knocked him off balance with her exuberant embrace. "Does this mean you'll escort me for the season?"

"At least the start of it." Orin held her at arm's length. Could this be his niece now grown so tall and so striking? "How can it be that you're ready for society or society ready for you? I seem to remember a lass in leading strings."

"Leading strings aside, I'm far more confident about my debut with you by my side." She smiled and flushed all at once, her features a pleasing blend of the Hedleys and the Humes. "Given you've spent several seasons in London, you have an expertise few do."

He looked to her discarded book by the window. "What were you reading when I rudely interrupted you?"

"Your interruption is far better than *Love in Excess*. I do wish you'd leave off writing poetry and plays and try your hand at a novel."

"I'm not having much success at anything literary at the moment." He took a seat near the hearth and faced an unfamiliar instrument by a window. "Mayhap your music will inspire me."

She clasped her hands together in that charming way he remembered. "Father ordered a pedal harp for my birthday after he refused to buy bagpipes."

He chuckled at her impudence. "Bagpipes are harder to play."

Gracefully, she sat by what could only be called an objet d'art, a large gilded instrument decorated with flowers and depictions of Minerva, the patroness of artists. Taking a deep breath, she tilted the harp then leaned it on her shoulder and began to gently pluck the strings.

Each ethereal note seemed to evoke an avalanche of shuttered memories, casting him back to that dark day. Hadn't Maryn played another harp in this very room before they all took to the sleighs? His gaze veered to a window. He'd sat in this very chair and looked out those same panes onto snow. How many times since he'd rued leaving his seat to follow the lure of that wintry world. If only he'd stayed put. Taken up a book. Ignored the challenge. Today he hadn't time to ruminate long as behind him came a rustle of silk and an unmistakable dulcet voice.

"Orin Alistair Cospatrick Hume, can it be you?"

A rush of warmth in his chest—and a beat of amusement that she used his full name—replaced the chill of before. He stood and faced the Countess of Wedderburn, torn between an embrace and a bow. Lady Blythe had an undeniable presence. He'd seen royalty less regal yet she exuded a genuineness royalty lacked.

"Milady," he said, giving a courtly bow.

Tears sprang to her eyes as she embraced him. "Welcome home."

The harp music continued, allowing them a private moment. He felt oddly emotional. This woman who'd wed his eldest brother had always been more mother to him than sister-in-law. Had he only been seven when she'd fled her Northumberland home and taken refuge at Wedderburn Castle?

"I've hoped and prayed you'd return to us at just the right time and here you are." She continued to study him as if accounting for the time they'd been apart. "The laird is out hawking but should return by supper."

"I hope you don't mind that I've brought a guest." His gaze swung to Charis. Matchmaker he was not, but he wanted her to have the domestic felicity he lacked. "Lord Lovell is upstairs but will join us for supper."

Blythe's delighted smile banished his concern. "An upstanding young gentleman is always welcome."

"None finer than Lord Lovell. I left the rakes behind in London." A great many libertines he didn't want anywhere near his lovely niece.

"We have a few rakes here though the laird doesn't let them trespass."

Another swing of the door and a maid entered with tea and toddies and the bannocks he'd missed but couldn't seem to find anywhere else. Charis left her harp and they sat in a companionable circle as more coal brought by a footman enlivened the hearth's fire.

"So tell us about your literary pursuits of late," the countess said, pouring tea.

"Or the lack of them," he replied bluntly.

Charis sent him a worried look. "Perhaps a change of scene will provide inspiration."

"You mentioned His Majesty's birthday in your last letter," Blythe said as he reached for a toddy. "I suppose that's a challenging endeavor given his choleric temper."

He grimaced. "I might not be the Poet Laureate much longer if I don't come up with something suitable."

"Perhaps you'll meet a lady who'll turn you so tapsalteerie that all your bottled-up musings will pour out." Charis gave a wink as she stirred milk and sugar into her teacup. "Once your homecoming is known, all the Lowlands will be a-titter."

Orin winked back at her. "This is your debut, not mine, remember."

She laughed as he took a bracing sip of the toddy, savoring the tang of whiskied cloves and nutmeg.

"Your enterprising uncle has brought a guest..." Blythe told her daughter between sips. "So it seems the social season has already begun."

Charis turned to him in question. "Oh?"

"Lord Lovell," Orin said.

A pause. "Here...in this very house?"

"Aye. He was in Edinburgh on business and we happened to meet up at the theatre a few nights ago. When he heard my plans he said he'd like to rekindle your acquaintance."

Charis's porcelain skin pinked. "Rekindle...what an interesting choice of word."

"His, not mine," Orin returned. "He's upstairs preparing to meet you."

Her hand went to her fair, upswept hair. "Then I'd best do the same and prepare to be met."

Blythe shook her head. "You look lovely as you are. 'Twill be interesting to hear of his adventures on the continent during his Grand Tour. You'll not want for conversation."

The reassurance seemed to settle her. Charis returned to her tea, though she kept her eye on the door as if Lord Lovell might walk through at any moment. Orin tempered his own hopes for a future match. People changed. Moved on. Grew apart. Few knew that truth as acutely as he did.

"Lovell's father is unwell and so he's begun to take on more of his affairs since returning to Britain." A dukedom wasn't to be taken lightly. Orin didn't envy him the title though Lovell was equal to the task. "The duke wishes to see his son wed before his passing."

"Well, he seems to have found an ally in you," Blythe told him with a sympathetic smile. "I wed your brother soon after your father passed despite the constraints of mourning. Grieving goes easier with a loving companion by your side."

"Is Lord Lovell much changed?" Charis asked. "'Tis been so long since we parted. And he is, if I recall, nine years older than I am."

"He's older, aye. Wiser," Orin said. "Isn't that the standard reply?"

"Indeed, Uncle." Charis rolled her eyes at his teasing. "Though I hate to appear overeager, supper does seem one too many hours away."

6

$\mathcal{A}$ letter came from Grandfather Lockhart in Edinburgh. Before she'd even read a word, the deterioration of his penmanship alerted her. Nearly eighty, he wasn't well. But at his great age, death was expected. And he would be the first in a long line of Lockharts to die of natural causes, apart from the *Lockhart curse*. For that Maryn could be thankful.

Taking a sunny seat by a window, she braced herself and broke the red seal bearing the ducal crest.

Dearest Granddaughter,

It was with great joy that I received your last letter. In my old age your frequent missives are my foremost pleasure. I rarely hear from your sister though I ken the reason. I do not hold her silence against her and I trust you do not either.

Maryn paused. She'd not seen her younger sister Nicola since the day that left them bereft and broken. Instead of begrudging her silence there was only a deep hurt. When Maryn missed her it was the Nicola of before, untouched by tragedy. If bitterness tried to take root over the fact Nicola lived in the next parish yet didn't visit, Maryn reminded herself she never bridged the distance either.

I delayed writing this letter in hopes of feeling better but alas, my physicians have told me to put my affairs in order. I do so now.

Maryn's mind spun. His heart condition?

I only ask that you oversee the display of a hatchment with our coat of arms upon it outside Lockhart Hall after my demise then hang it up on the wall of the Great Hall once mourning is complete. Funeral plans are proceeding as I decline.

How much longer did he have?

At present I am too ill to leave Edinburgh and my attending physicians nor do I want you to travel here. Let our remembrances of each other be of happier days till we reach heaven.

Your ever loving grandfather

A new sort of pain rent her. He was suffering. Without close kin at hand. Though she and Grandfather didn't see each other often just knowing he was there always assuaged her. But if she did lose him—and what was life but a series of losses large and small? —her peace was that God took him and named the very hour of his passing.

She refolded the letter. The next post might well bear the mournful black seal and plunge her into mourning again. On the other hand, she had a vast array of mourning garments in her wardrobe, beginning with the death of her dear grandmother, the duchess.

"I finished mending yer lilac lustring," Rosemary was saying from across the room. "'Tis good as new now."

Maryn pocketed the letter and looked up to see the maid holding a cascade of glossy silk and lace. "Best pack it for I'm to go to Edinburgh."

"Mercy, milady! Edinburgh?" Rosemary's eyes grew round as French buttons. "Ye've not left this cottage in years."

"All that is about to change since Grandfather Lockhart is unwell. I don't suppose you could accompany me. I'll pay twice your wages—"

"Losh! Nae need, truly. 'Tis a grave matter and I'm honored to do it." She began putting away her sewing. "When do we leave? I'll send word to the stables to ready a coach."

"In the morning then. I sense there's no time to waste."

In the spring, Edinburgh's stench and smoke was unleashed from winter's lockdown. Holding handkerchiefs to their noses, Maryn stepped down from the coach onto unfamiliar cobbles, Rosemary in her wake. Queasy from the long ride, she swallowed down the bile that had caught at the back of her throat since their journey began. How odd everything looked. So much color and confusion in the city after her cloistered existence in the countryside.

Her gaze rose to the towering tenement known as Lockhart's Land with its lofty eight stories. Her grandfather lived at the very top away from the foul wynds and closes below but surely all these steps couldn't be good for his heart. Hume's Land was also here somewhere on the High Street though it was the clan's elegant Canongate mansion at the bottom of the hill that she most remembered.

The ten o'clock drum resounded, calling all residents to retire. Their own courtyard in the Lawnmarket was soon locked. Up they climbed, a manservant hefting Maryn's trunk, all of them pausing at intervals to keep from gasping for breath. At last they reached the top, their reward a star-swept night, lights from Lady Stair's, their nearest neighbor, gilding the darkness.

"Och, milady!" Grandfather's longtime housekeeper failed to suppress her shock at their unexpected arrival. "Ye're in the nick o' time."

But alas, divested of her wraps, Maryn hastened down the hall too late despite their hurtling across the Lowlands. A physician by the bedside was just closing Grandfather's eyes. In that moment he seemed younger. Less lined. Maryn sensed he was at peace. Still, she wept, the late hour and her exhaustion making their final farewell a blur.

"My deepest apologies, Your Grace," the doctor said, withdrawing from the chamber.

Your Grace. Her new title was not lost on her. What had Grandfather done? No time to question. For the moment all she knew was a widening, gaping lonesomeness. Alone with him, Maryn took his thin, dry hand and clasped it like she'd done since she was wee. Only she was no longer wee. She was nearing thirty. And in one irrevocable moment she'd become, to her astonishment, a duchess.

That night she slept fitfully, more aware of her future than she'd ever been. The next morn while Grandfather was being prepared for burial, Maryn ventured on to the High Street in search of mourning gloves. She could have sent a servant but chose to do the deed herself. The city was a stranger to her so she went about in a sedan chair carried by two strapping Highlanders, the best of bodyguards. Her own infirmity seemed to make them more protective of her, that and the fact she was wearing black.

"What do you buy, madam?" the glover asked as she entered.

"Gloves to distribute as funeral gifts," she said without elaboration.

One hundred kid leather gloves later, she couldn't help but admire the lovely caps and hair ornaments outside a millinery and a wealth of fabric gracing the draper's bow windows. A perfumer tempted with beautiful scent bottles but it was the *Pot and Pineapple* that lured her inside. Boxes of sweetmeats and candied orange peel for the Edinburgh servants along with a cookbook for Rosemary lifted her spirits, after which she returned to Lockhart's Land.

Sunlight banished the early morning mist and steadied her enough to make funeral arrangements and prepare for the reading of the will. The executor of the estate was none other than Lord Stair, their attorney neighbor.

"I've been charged with the proper and lawful handling of the late duke's estate along with several barristers and solicitors of renowned legal expertise . . . which sounds quite cold and administrative given your grandfather was a close personal friend."

"For which I'm very grateful," Maryn told him from the mahogany confines of Grandfather's study.

"The duke asked for a quiet, simple burial. No ceremony or lying-in state. His body is to be interred in your family's vault at Ladykirk. Berwick nobles, family members, associates, and household servants are invited to attend the funeral once the death announcement is made and a date decided." He cleared his throat. "I shall notify your kin directly once you've given me their names and whereabouts."

"My sister Nicola, Lady Marchmont, at Redbraes Castle in the shire of Berwick."

"Any others, Your Grace?"

Maryn bit her lip. "A few distant relations beyond the Lowlands who are little more than strangers to me."

"Very well. I shall send word to Redbraes then. Will you be returning to Lockhart Hall to inform the servants?"

She'd not considered this amid the suddenness of it all. But duties must be observed. The servants who'd served them so faithfully shouldn't be informed by anyone other than family. "I shall do so on the morrow."

"Once that is done, please send word to me about the reading of the will. I can come to Lockhart Hall, of course, at your bidding."

"Preferable, thank you." Her gaze swept the mostly unfamiliar chamber. "I'll need to decide what's to be done with this tenement. I suppose rather than displace tenants I should leave it be for now."

"Wise, Your Grace. This structure has been in your family for generations and is quite convenient when you're in the city."

Maryn made a mental list of all that needed to be done as he continued on.

"I'll take care of settling taxes and any outstanding debts here in Edinburgh and elsewhere. Your grandfather's estate is quite complex and will take considerable time for you to comprehend though there is no question that you hold the Duchy of Fordyce. Given your twin brother's death, your Scottish title has been granted with remainder to pass to you rather than falling into abeyance."

Herschel. Her beloved brother's absence cut especially deep at such a time. He should be standing here, hale and hearty, not her. She felt akin to an imposter, a usurper. Herschel William Henry Lockhart would have made a splendid duke.

Lord Stair concluded, "If your line is to die out, the title might become extinct or pass to a relative."

If. She was definitely in danger of that with no suitors in sight. Maryn thanked him, wanting nothing more than a quiet corner and a simple bowl of brose and a crust of bread, as if it could clear her muddled head.

7

$\int$eeing Charis and Lord Lovell together almost made a skeptic believe in enduring love. The supper hour passed with only the laird and Blythe—another obvious and enduring love match—Charis, Lovell, and himself. A fifth wheel, if you will. After a dessert of fern cakes, they all went outside to the formal gardens as the evening was so fair.

Charis and her suitor wandered down a graveled path to a reflecting pool while the laird kept to the terrace, his walking stick in hand.

"Is your auld war wound ailing you?" Orin asked, going no further than the terrace's iron railing.

"Aye, though this vantage point makes me forget it," Everard said with a patient smile as Blythe came to stand by his side.

Together the three of them looked out over parterres whose hedges and flowers formed an intricate pattern as they descended to a pond brimming with white water lilies. Here they had an enviable view of Berwickshire and Charis, too.

"Our daughter's season might be short lived," Lady Blythe said wistfully, "though the opening ball is almost upon us."

"Which is when?" Orin asked.

"The second of June. Invitations have been sent and it seems all of Berwickshire will attend."

The laird looked at him knowingly. "Are you prepared for such a reunion?"

"Meaning I may cause as much a stir as Charis?"

"Something like that," Everard said. "Best prepare yourself."

Orin fixed his gaze on a flock of black-faced sheep grazing in the distance. "I suppose my appearance will remind many of what happened."

Everard nodded. "Five years isn't fifty, so it's still fresh."

"I doubt any of our guests will speak of it," Blythe said, the faint lines in her face deepening. "Even those closest to the tragedy."

A pained hush followed and into the gap rushed a host of unwanted images. Cold snow. Bright blood. The eerie sound of sleigh bells in a sudden blast of wind. Orin's gaze veered east to the harrowing site he couldn't see, miles distant. The majestic if scarred oak tree still stood, he guessed, the rush of watery burn beneath.

He finally said, "I'm most concerned about the Lockharts."

"None are on the guest list," Blythe told him. "Simply because the Duke of Fordyce—who is said to be ailing—resides in Edinburgh and Lady Nicola, née Marchmont, rarely leaves Redbraes Castle."

Orin looked at her in question. "What of Lady Maryn?"

"She seems to have…" Blythe raised her hands in a sort of resignation—"vanished."

Orin felt an odd tightening in his chest, his hands fisted upon the terrace's rail.

She continued slowly, "After that tragic day, the duke is said to have taken her to the city for medical treatment. From what I've gathered, Lady Nicola married as soon as mourning allowed and has since been busy raising a family. Lockhart Hall remains empty save the servants and an occasional visit from Fordyce."

Orin swallowed past the knot in his throat. "I tried to contact Lady Maryn by letter." More than one. Mayhap a half dozen. Finally he'd reconciled himself to the fact there would be no reply.

Blythe looked as grieved as he felt. "No one seems to know anything about her, though there is speculation aplenty. Some believe she was too injured to appear in public after. Some have even guessed a nervous breakdown."

Ire and anguish twisted inside him once again, making him rue his part in that day with all its unseen repercussions. "I could ride to Redbraes and find out." It wasn't the first time he'd considered it.

"Akin to riding into battle, resurrecting auld wounds," the laird warned. As a former soldier awarded the Order of the Thistle for chivalry, his words held particular punch.

"There are servants still at Lockhart Hall, then," Orin said, wanting to get the facts right.

"A closed-mouthed few," Blythe answered.

"I've even considered contacting the duke in Edinburgh, but given I'm responsible for the death of his heir—"

"You're not responsible," Lady Blythe said at once, "though you may feel so, caring as you do."

"I was older–and should have been wiser."

Everard took hold of his walking stick again. "It was naught but a spur-of-the-moment accident brought about by a number of unfortunate factors."

"By reason of a careless bet and weather I knew better than to hazard." Orin's voice shook though he tried to steady it.

"In hindsight, perhaps," the laird said quietly but firmly. "At five and twenty foresight is often lacking."

The approach to Lockhart Hall was one Maryn had often made with her twin brother on horseback. Herschel was a renowned equestrian who'd even published a work on horsemanship with engraved plates prior to his passing. She kept a treasured copy to read when she missed him most, feeling she heard an eternal echo of his voice in his carefully penned words.

"Might ye be a tad unweel, Yer Grace?" Across from her, Rosemary's concern returned her to the tumultuous present.

"Ah, the rigors of coach-riding..." Maryn searched her pocket for smelling salts. Pungent peppermint perfumed the air, calming her roiling stomach if not her nerves.

Finally, fifty miles of queasiness was coming to a blessed end. Uppermost in Maryn's mind was another feeling entirely. This was the first time she'd come to Lockhart Hall as something other than a daughter or granddaughter. Scales seemed to fall from her eyes as she saw the house and grounds from a different perspective. This resplendent place which she'd never once considered hers befitted a proper duchess, not a recluse who found comfort in an obscure cottage.

"I must tell the servants straightaway," she murmured.

Rosemary looked on sympathetically. "'Tis a melancholy business."

But there were few servants to tell—a butler nearly as old as Grandfather, a silver-haired housekeeper stooped with age, four maids, two footmen, and a cook reeking of rum. Maryn shared the news as gently as she could, leaving the dour lot of them wondering about their own fate.

"Would you like your former room readied, Your Grace?" the housekeeper asked as the sonorous hall clock chimed seven.

Maryn wanted nothing more than her familiar box bed but the servants were looking so dejected she felt compelled to stay. "That would be most welcome, Mrs. Duncan. Thank you."

Dawn broke with birdsong, rousing Maryn long before first light. Finches. Starlings. Sparrows. Blackbirds. Robins. All joined in a symphony beyond her unshuttered windows. For a moment her strange circumstances righted. Living far away from any grandeur had heightened her appreciation of the natural world. If she decided to move to Lockhart Hall would she lose those simple joys amid all her new duties?

Waiting till her bedchamber grew light, she got up and rang the little bell on her dressing table that summoned Rosemary from the adjoining room.

"I'm glad to be on hand," Rosemary told her, selecting a black fringed linen gown. "And though it may be irreverent to say, sable is a bonny compliment to yer eyes and complexion."

So much sable. Alas, her hair was so black it held blue, Grandfather always said, much like her late grandmother's. The proof of their likeness was on the Portrait Gallery wall. Maryn shared Herschel's moss green eyes though his hair had been a lighter hue.

Peering into the looking glass mirror, she gave a pinch to her pale cheeks, which only seemed to magnify the fact that she was befreckled.

In the dressing room, Rosemary examined a pair of clocked stockings and garters. "If ye're needing a proper lady's maid I'd be pleased to live here at Lockhart Hall."

Would she? Maryn considered this. "You'd not mind staying nights? Your Sabbaths would still be free."

"Now that my brothers and sisters aren't so wee, my mam and da can spare me. Besides," Rosemary brightened. "Whoever thought a simple Berwick lass could be in service to a duchess?"

A most unusual duchess. Maryn tried not to look at her maimed limb, a telltale reminder of all that had gone before. Despite Grandfather's best hopes and the doctor's best efforts, little could be done. Her left arm and hand hung limply by her side though it no longer pained her unless there was a change of weather.

Give thanks through the hurt.

The London surgeon's unwelcome words back then had lifted her over many a bump since. She pondered it now while Rosemary left to find the housekeeper and breakfast.

Maryn went below to the dining room with its many windows and just as many memories. Like curtains parting, dawn beckoned her to look outside. Meticulously cultivated topiaries and flower beds and hedges bespoke full-time gardeners. Her gaze roamed, savoring the details she'd missed. The grounds, mostly unchanged since her childhood, seemed a step back in time like the great house. A shame few enjoyed it. Had Grandfather made any alterations since she and Herschel had lived here with him after their parents' passing?

Served a breakfast of smoked salmon, oatcakes, summerhouse strawberries, and tea, Maryn finished and visited the mansion room by room, starting in the marbled entrance hall with its black-and-white tiled floor. A cherry red drawing room—her favorite in childhood—was opposite the Prussian blue dining room. The large library was a delight to any reader—again a shame that it sat idle. Through a second door in the library was Grandfather's cabinet, a circular room of blue damask and many windows ideal for deskwork. For a moment she stood atop the chamber's Persian rug, a timeworn purple and grey, and tried to feel at home without all the … ghosts.

Mrs. Duncan appeared suddenly, startling her. "I had a fire lit to chase away the chill of the morning. When in residence, this is where your late grandfather spent most of his time."

"Thank you. 'Tis where I most remember him. Little seems to have changed."

"Very little, other than refurbished servants' quarters for which we're very thankful. For most of us this has been our home for many a year."

Maryn mulled what she remembered about the tiny woman before her. A learned woman who could read. Who'd never married but had a talent for housekeeping and all its many facets.

"We dinna ken where we'd go otherwise."

"That shan't alter," Maryn reassured her. "I hope that you'll bring me any needs or concerns you or any of the servants have."

"Does that mean you're staying on?" A beat of hope enlivened her words.

Maryn tried to smile but would make no promises. "At least till the funeral and the reading of the will. Expect a huddle of legal men in future."

Mrs. Duncan withdrew and Maryn returned to her study of the cabinet now bathed in brighter light. Grandfather's interest and preferences were everywhere, from the maps of the Americas on the walls to leatherbound books in glass-fronted cases.

A portrait of a young Grandmother Lockhart hung above the mantel, painted at the time of her marriage. The duchess's tiara sparkled in the ray of sun shining upon it, a reminder of the Lockhart jewels. Maryn hadn't a clue where they were nor had she the slightest urge to wear them though they'd held her spellbound as a child.

Feeling like a trespasser, she sat at the ornate oak desk with cabriole legs as another cob-webbed memory shook loose. Long ago, Grandfather had hidden sweets in various compartments of this very desk, including a secret drawer she'd forgotten how to access. Her right hand ran over the smooth wood like they once had the pianoforte's ivory keys. So many odd brass knobs within and without.

At the back of the desk she fingered a carved fleur-de-lis and instinctively pressed its ornate design. An accompanying click was followed by her gasp as it opened, revealing a velvet-lined space secreting an abundance of intriguing things. Velvet pouches, old keys, foreign coins, ornate wax seals, and yellowed letters tied with faded silk ribbon.

Nary a single sweetmeat.

Nostalgia overtook her at the scent of aged wood and beeswax and ink. Such an ancient desk rife with history, even mystery. Still feeling a trespasser, she started to shut the drawer when her gaze fell on the topmost letter. Face down, it bore an unbroken, silver wax seal she knew all too well.

A crest featuring a hand holding a sword within a heart. *Fidelis ad finum.* True to the end. The Hume family motto.

Could it be? *Nay,* her head said. *Aye,* shouted her heart. Her fingers pulled at the silk ribbon binding them and half a dozen letters spilled into her lap. Each addressed to Lady Maryn Lockhart of Lockhart Hall. Old, unread letters, every seal intact.

The bittersweet discovery gave way to a jumble of long denied feelings as bewilderment rushed in.

From Orin Hume?

Her childhood friend who delighted like no other. The one whose presence lit up a room. And whose absence still tore her in two.

8

*O*rin arrived at Ladykirk a bit late on purpose. News of the ailing Duke of Fordyce's death hadn't been unexpected but still caught the Humes by surprise. A sizeable crowd thronged the kirkyard as the nobleman was laid to rest. Eyes down, he kept to the fringes though he was the tallest of the Humes, a generous inch over the laird, his eldest, tallest brother. Everard stood not far from him with Lady Blythe and Charis.

The tattered clouds above, pushed along by a warm wind, resurrected another startlingly similar day. Odd what one remembered. He'd been seven at his father's funeral. Someone had brought flowers. Lilies? His nurse had slipped candied peel into his pocket. He'd been peely-wally as a lad and so the newly minted laird had had to carry him all the way back to Wedderburn Castle.

The minister's hoarse voice returned him to the present. All bowed their heads as a prayer was said. Several women near him were murmuring after the amen. About the Lockhart curse?

"Look at her, poor lass."

"I dinna care that she's a duchess now. She's poor as Job's turkey with nae kinfolk."

"She's not been seen in these parts for many a year. I do wonder what will become of the Hall..."

Orin averted his gaze from the coffin to allow any of the Lockharts privacy at so poignant a time. But at the mention of no family members he looked over the crowd to the lass in question.

Lady Maryn stood by the casket clad head to toe in black, a veil obscuring her face. A white rose dangled from one hand. A nod to the duke's Jacobite sympathies? Did she not ken observing the allegiance might well place her in jeopardy?

His gaze held as the service ended and she turned away, climbing into the waiting Lockhart coach and vanishing again. Two of her liveried servants remained, passing out the customary gift of funeral gloves.

"Did you see Lady Maryn?" Charis asked once they returned to Wedderburn Castle, gloves in hand. "If only we could have spoken with her–offered our condolences in person."

Orin was still at a loss for words.

They gathered in the family drawing room, just he, the laird and Blythe, and Charis. Lord Lovell's father had sent for him and so he had left for their estate in Yorkshire, his return for the opening ball of the season unlikely. A maidservant brought drinks. Tea for the ladies and whisky for the men. Orin took a bracing sip as he stood to one side of the hearth.

"I suppose we would have had to strike her from the ball's guest list given she's in mourning again," Lady Blythe said. "Yet what she needs is company. Merriment to help ease her at such a time."

"Odd that there's nae lykewake." Everard took a seat, no doubt remembering his own father's burial. "Nae feasting and dancing."

Blythe shook her head. "Reverend Percival said the duke expressly stated there was to be none of that, though it defies Scottish tradition. I'm guessing he wanted to spare Lady Maryn."

"Did Percival say anything else?" Orin looked at his sister-in-law, who surely knew the heart of his query.

Lady Maryn's whereabouts, for one.

"Very little. Just that the family requests privacy at this time."

"Which is nae different than any other time," the laird said bluntly.

Maryn returned to Lockhart Hall following the funeral to find an unfamiliar coach and four at the stables and a dismayed look on Mrs. Duncan's face.

"Your Grace, they arrived once you departed for Ladykirk . . . all five of them."

Five? Bone-tired, Maryn fought dismay as she removed her hat and veil in the tiled hall. "And who might they be?"

"Lord and Lady Marchmont." The housekeeper gestured to the open door of the formal drawing room. "And your wee nieces."

I didna ken I had any.

Maryn stood turned to stone. Her merry-go-round of emotions now included mortification.

Mrs. Duncan continued with more composure. "I supplied them with refreshments and made them as comfortable as I could."

Prior to the funeral, her sister hadn't sent word whether she was coming or not, adding more uncertainty to the day. Maryn murmured a silent prayer that was more plea and forced herself forward with as much strength and dignity as she could muster.

Her guests stood with a flurry of curtseying and a formal bow, reminding her once more of her new standing. In the ensuing silence the five year absence seemed like an abyss neither sister was willing to cross.

"Your Grace ... " Lord Marchmont began, " ... pardon our unexpected arrival."

Maryn tried to smile at the suitor who'd pursued and won her sister's hand. But their nuptials, far from being the grand affair of Nicola's dreams, had shrunk to a rushed, secretive ceremony shadowed by tragedy. Maryn hadn't even attended given she was under medical care for months.

Alas, time had not been kind to Lord Marchmont. Balding and pockmarked, he was not only older but clearly unwell. Nicola, on the other hand, was bonnier than ever, even in black.

"Please have a seat," Maryn said then realized her error. Having sat so long, mightn't they benefit from a walk in the gardens, the children especially?

Three little girls in matching petticoats stared back at her, the eldest pointing at the portrait of a medieval duchess behind Maryn. "Why are you not wearing your crown?"

"Hush, Charlotte," Nicola told her. "You're to address your aunt as *Your Grace* henceforth."

"Please ... " Maryn said quickly, soaking in the sight of her fetching nieces. "Aunt Maryn shall be fine in future."

Provided I ever see you again.

She lingered on her eldest niece who bore a remarkable resemblance to Nicola. The flaxen-haired girl had the telltale Lockhart coloring and green eyes while the other two sisters were dark as Maryn herself.

"Your daughters are lovely," she said. "What are their names?"

For a trice Nicola seemed pleased. "Charlotte is the eldest at almost six and is named after our mother. Penelope—Pen, we call her—is four, and Eugenie is two. If we have a son he's to be called Herschel."

A son? Was she expecting? On that poignant note they passed through a French door to the formal garden where the girls began winging about like uncaged birds.

"We came for the reading of the will," Lord Marchmont said, hat in hand.

"Rather we got the funeral mixed up with the will's reading," Nicola corrected.

Maryn put her hand on the terrace's balustrade, eyes on their mother's namesake. How proud she'd be. All three were delightfully unique. Their happy chatter and laughter helped ease the mounting tension.

"We won't stay but felt it prudent to remain long enough to ask about the will," Nicola said.

"Grandfather's solicitors and such will be here in a sennight," Maryn told them, naming the date. Did her uneasiness about the matter show?

"We shall return then," Lord Marchmont said, bending his gaunt form to sit on a near bench.

Nicola stayed standing, sunlight calling out the deep crease in her brow. "You may know that Grandfather and I didn't part on the best of terms."

Maryn raked her mind for the cause of their dissension and came up empty. "If you and Grandfather were at odds I've no recollection of it."

"You were still recovering and ignorant of what ensued. I've no wish to speak of it now nor recall that dreadful time ever again."

For once they were in agreement. But try as she might, Maryn couldn't shut the door on the past.

"We must put all that behind us." Nicola's voice held that high aggrieved note she'd never liked. "'Tis exceedingly difficult to see

you today, partly because we've not spoken since the tragedy."
She waved a gloved hand about. "Everything here echoes and
screams of loss. Mother and Father should still be with us if not
Grandfather. And Herschel, most definitely. This is all his as heir."

Shaken, Maryn sat on a bench opposite her brother-in-law
whose eyes were closed as if napping. The sunlight failed to
warm her and seemed to illuminate all that was wrong with
their fractious situation.

"I fail to understand how you even attended the funeral,"
Nicola went on. "Facing all of Berwickshire after all that has
happened."

"I had no choice." Maryn fisted a handkerchief in her lap. As
it was, she'd kept her eyes down throughout the short, somber
service and didn't have the presence of mind to even take in
who'd attended or who hadn't. "I needed to honor Grandfather
a final time."

Nicola's tone turned more exasperated. "Well, I'm sure
everyone from here to Edinburgh is now resurrecting the
Lockhart curse."

"Superstitions abound, my dear," Lord Marchmont chimed
in. "And never more than in Scotland. Such can't be helped."

"We're not the only family who's suffered misfortune,"
Maryn said quietly.

"At least death spared Hershel any injuries such as yours."
Nicola fixed her attention on Maryn's injured, gloved arm with
such revulsion it might have been a pirate's hook instead.

Swallowing down a bitter retort borne of hurt, Maryn traded
the terrace for the garden, on the heels of the girls chasing a butterfly as it flitted about the fountain. When Eugenie fell, Maryn
righted her, rewarded with a gap-toothed smile.

Charlotte let her little sisters go ahead and lagged behind
with Maryn. "Mama says you're my aunt. What does that make
me?"

"Since I'm your mother's sister, you're my niece."

"Are 'Genie and Pen your nieces too?"

"Yes, all three of you."

"Why haven't we seen you before?"

"Your mother has been very busy bringing up a family."

"Do you have any children we can play with?"

"Nay."

"Why not?"

Out of the mouths of babes.

Penelope spared her an answer when she asked, "Can I pick some flowers for Mama?"

"Of course." Maryn gestured to freesia and waxflowers around them. "Whatever you wish ... but careful, the roses have thorns."

The showy, fragrant phlox was far safer and Penelope picked a fistful, running all the way back to the terrace in a touching bid to please her mother.

Charlotte slipped her small, soft hand into Maryn's as they followed. "I do hope we can come back here."

As do I.

Suddenly choked, Maryn said nothing, wishing all rifts could be mended and tragedies undone.

9

June arrived with as much inspiration as Scotland could muster. Amid the lush green in every direction, Orin spent time hawking and riding with the laird, content to lay down his pen but for the unwelcome reminder of the king's birthday. He countered this with thoughts of how to bring books to the Lowlands but thus far he hadn't any idea how to begin. The prospect seemed overwhelming yet whet his determination to see it done.

For now, the social season loomed. Wedderburn Castle's ball was a day away and the servants were busy transforming the public rooms into spotless, fragrant bowers by bringing in the outdoors. More crystal vases than he could count adorned the space, waiting for cut flowers from both garden and summerhouse.

Lord Lovell hadn't returned but Charis seemed too preoccupied to dwell on his absence. Dressmakers and milliners came and went with all their colorful goods. Daughters were expensive, Orin decided. Moreso than sons.

"Is this your entire trousseau or simply dresses for the season?" he teased his niece after finding her in the family drawing room in a rare idle moment.

She smiled. "Perhaps both."

"As for me, I believe I've brought my tailored best." But he wasn't sure as he had no manservant to confirm. What he wore or anyone else wore for that matter had never concerned him till now.

With a sigh, Charis bit her lip. "My fear is that you'll find us a rustic backwater after London's drawing rooms."

"Refreshing, rather." He had few fond memories of society. "Protocol is stifling."

"Needs be I ponder something other than this debut." She sat at a table spread with newspapers and magazines. "Have you read the latest issue of *Tatler*?"

"Nay, but something tells me you have."

"You forgot to point out it contains a bit of your own verse."

"Hardly worth mentioning."

"I beg to differ..." She began thumbing through the magazine. "There's another worthy here who caught my eye called *the one-armed poet*."

"Another anonymous writer afraid to pen their own name?" Orin took a chair across from her. "There's a rash of them."

"Do you know of any poet missing an appendage?"

"Nary a one." He took the magazine from her and read a stanza. Pretty. Witty. Even elegant. And startlingly familiar—or was he only imagining it? It made the dry well of his own creativity even drier. He feigned disinterest.

She took back the paper. "I saw you coming out of the tower. Inspiration abounds there, I hope."

"The auld library always draws me."

"Father has threatened to tear it down but Mama won't hear of it since it was her place of refuge during the rebellion."

"Where she was secreted after fleeing England, aye. And where I discovered her after originally believing her to be a water kelpie in the garden."

"A charming story."

"I side with your mother about preserving the place and attest your father is more sentimental than he appears."

"Beneath that gruff soldierly exterior lies a tender heart, yes. I ken my leaving will go hard on him as the only daughter."

He winked. "Only till you bring home grandchildren."

She smiled and crossed her arms, just like the laird would do. An unladylike pose, though Charis was thoroughly ladylike. "I want you to pray Lord Lovell back."

He chuckled despite the sudden soreness in his chest. "The Almighty and I are not on the best terms lately."

"Oh?" Compassion shone on her lovely face. Charis had the rare faith of a child.

"God seems... distant," he admitted.

"God never moves, Uncle. You are too much in the world, perhaps."

Was he? He loathed London. Mayhap there was the rub as Shakespeare said.

"Mama says there are seasons of life." She looked at him searchingly. "Perhaps 'tis a change you need, and I'm not talking about a social season."

His gaze swung to a window, the day beckoning them outdoors. He should go for a ride. Clear his head. Not confide in Charis as an equal when she was his much younger niece.

"What do you wish for, Uncle Orin?"

"Wish for?" A fanciful question. "I ken what I don't wish for—the city. I want to live far from London and Edinburgh and surround myself with books."

"As a lonely bachelor?"

"Nay. Society hasn't pushed me that far. I not only want to surround myself with books, I want to make books available to others." The more he entertained the notion the more firmly it took hold of him. If he pursued that ambition he could more easily bow out of being Poet Laureate. Forsake England altogether.

"You're ready to return to Scotland, sounds like. I overheard Father offer you one of his lesser properties—or the gatehouse."

"The gatehouse full of ghosts."

She laughed. "No one's lived there since Grandmother's lady's companion half a century ago." She tugged at his sleeve. "Let's go have a look, shall we?"

Maryn sat in the now familiar chair at the now familiar desk in Grandfather's cabinet. The round chamber was at its best bathed in light. Now almost summer, crimson blooms smothered the upper windowpanes as climbing roses reached summer heights. But it was the desk that drew her ... or rather the letters.

A low fire burned in the grate, enough of a blaze to burn the stack of letters that gave her no rest. No need to read them, just be rid of them and thereby close the door on the past with such finality it could never be reopened.

Quickly, lest she change her mind, Maryn pulled the handle of the main drawer, reached to the back for the fleur-de-lis and pressed it, springing the lock. Letters in hand, she got up and went to the hearth, a marvel of marble that momentarily distracted her with its ornate cupids and festoons of flowers. Pressing the letters to her bodice in a moment of angst, she extended the stack to the flames.

And then snatched them back.

Indecision pummeled her. Worse than burning them was never knowing what Orin had said. But old as they were, what did it matter?

Pulling the topmost letter free of the ribbon tie—were they in order?—she secreted the rest in their hiding place. Her fingers nearly shook as she broke the seal. Five years had faded the ink and deeply creased the paper.

17 December, 1735

Dear Maryn,

Mayhap I should address you by your title of lady but in truth, we are long past any formalities. I'll cut to the heart of the matter and say I shall never be the same for Herschel's loss nor absolve myself of my part in his death nor your injuries. For the rest of my life I will want to turn back time and take away that rash moment and spare you and your family the shattering consequences. I can neither forgive myself nor ask for your forgiveness. All I can offer are a few broken-hearted sentences here.

> *Your entire,*
> *Orin Hume*

The words blurred and Maryn blinked back tears. The carefree life they'd once shared had been lost to them. There was no returning to it. And no logical reason to cling to the letters.

10

The gatehouse had intrigued him since childhood. One of Orin's earliest memories was of his beloved mother bringing him here. Why, he didn't recall. Something about the particular species of roses that grew in the walled garden but refused to bloom in the more formal gardens of the castle or elsewhere.

Later it had been his and Maryn's trysting place in the most innocent of ways. The abandoned haunt had become a stage, the setting Verona, Italy, and the two of them Romeo and Juliet, first reading their parts, then memorizing them. Sometimes she would leave him letters in the garden's stone wall.

But he wouldn't tell Charis that.

"Look!" she exclaimed as they walked around the high wall to the gatehouse's noble exterior. In front was the dusty road to Duns. "Have you ever seen such blooms? Nearly the size of dinner plates and the scent is divine..."

Fragrant blush roses framed a white wooden doorway, begging a gardener's pruning. Moss and ivy grew in green profusion across the gray stone, covering the arched windows. Orin took out the key the laird had given him. The door shuddered and groaned from years of disuse as he pushed it open and they passed beneath the lintel. He left it ajar for fresh air.

"I didn't realize the place was so bare." Charis began to move about the entrance hall, a miniature of Wedderburn Castle with its tiled foyer and tapestries. The stairway's banister was whitened with dust, light from a transom window pouring in and exposing every crack and crevice.

"How many rooms did Father say were here?" she asked him.

"Parlor. Dining room. Study. Two bedchambers. Kitchen and larder."

Carpets a century old still retained their vivid hues since few feet had trod them. Spiderwebs glinted in the low beams brushing Orin's head. He waved his cocked hat to dispel them, gaze resting on the painting over the mantel. The first earl of Wedderburn stared back at him, a forbidding figure in medieval attire. Those hawkish eyes seemed to follow them as painted subjects often did, chilling his overly imaginative mind.

"Perhaps your muse could meet you here," Charis said, examining a desk below the largest window. "You may feel more a guest at the castle but this gatehouse could be yours entirely. Nary a servant to intrude on your solitude unless needed. And if you crave company you could continue to take your meals with us."

How inviting she made it sound. His gaze traveled to the maddeningly bare bookshelves framing the parlor fireplace. Had the former occupant not been a reader? "An agreeable proposition."

"There's plenty of furnishings in storage to choose from. You could even move your favorites from Hume House in London. But first, a thorough cleaning is in order."

They went upstairs, the views expansive. He wondered how the light would fall at dawn and dusk, the most hallowed times of days. By the time they passed out the back door into the walled garden his decision had been made.

Charis pulled a watch from her pocket. "I promised Mama I'd return for tea."

"Go ahead then. I'll tarry a few minutes more."

Color and scent overwhelmed him. Someone had kept the garden free of weeds, at least. Flowers were everywhere. Alone, he sat upon the bench where he'd once stood, spouting lines and trying not to laugh.

For never was a story of more woe than this of Juliet and her Romeo.

Unless it was Lady Maryn and Orin Hume.

As for her ladyship, Maryn had preferred to stay on the ground or circle the fountain in sun, rain, or snow. His gaze swung to the font in question. Had it broken? Its basin held wind-whipped leaves and flower petals but little water. Directly in back of it was that unique niche in the wall—

Dinna look, man.

The caution lasted a trice then look he did. It was impossible to ignore that part of the wall with the heart carved in stone near the rear gate. It allowed for someone to slip inside and leave a letter in the wall's crevice. To his knowledge, only he and Maryn had ever used it. A tug of curiosity and sentiment pulled him closer. She'd never responded to any of his letters after the accident. Unless...

He walked the garden's perimeter, past heirloom flowers he had no name for, daring to hope. Daring to believe after all this time and all this weather a piece of paper might be waiting, sealed with the wax he remembered. Blue wax bearing a rose. His hands felt the rough stone, fingers wedging themselves inside the slight opening. He steeled himself against the avalanche of disappointment.

The crevice was empty. Empty as his pulsing heart.

Orin found himself tolerating the season's opening ball. Partly because Lord Lovell had returned and he felt less adrift amid the sea of faces, unfamiliar and familiar. And partly because Charis seemed to be enjoying herself immensely.

Especially when playing matchmaker.

"Uncle, allow me to introduce Miss Ivory Lyon." The tap of Charis's fan on his arm claimed his full attention.

He gave a slight bow and faced the most flawless lass he'd ever seen as Charis continued, "Miss Lyon resides near the ruins of Hume Castle. She and her family are somewhat new to the Borders."

He met a pair of lively hazel eyes and wondered exactly where in the Borders. And when. He used to know all of Berwickshire.

"At Lyon Court," the lass in question said with an equally flawless smile. "Perhaps you've heard of it or if not would like to make its acquaintance." Her words were low and sultry. Inviting.

He searched for some flaw—something to say—and came up empty.

"Being accomplished equestrians, you two might well meet out riding on the Merse," Charis said in his stead.

Beyond Charis's shoulder the laird was looking on—and looking amused. Was he privy to his daughter's schemes?

"May I have the pleasure of a dance?" Orin asked as the music began.

Both Charis and Miss Lyon seemed pleased. He'd shunned the opening minuet in favor of a longways dance he could step in his sleep. Outside of etiquette-heavy London and the Court, he enjoyed dancing. Scottish ballrooms were more earthy than elevated.

Miss Lyon obliged, earning the obvious admiration of many an onlooker in the room. She danced flawlessly too and she was even wearing his favorite shade of blue. His initial reserve began to thaw just as perspiration dampened his lip. Miss Lyon did not perspire one whit, nor did she seem winded after several sets.

"Are you at Wedderburn Castle for long, Mr. Hume?" she asked as they partnered again.

"For the season," he replied.

"Your niece told me you've taken up residence in the gatehouse. A charming structure."

"I prefer it to the city."

"Country life suits us both, then."

They circled and faced outwards, finally stepping back to each other as a dozen couples swirled on both sides of them. For a moment, he forgot them all.

"You're at home near Hume Castle then," he said.

"For the past two years, yes. Mother's health is delicate and so Father moved us from Glasgow in hopes the country air might revive her. We have Berwick kinfolk. The Kerrs."

A longstanding Lowland clan. Well respected land owners and the like.

"I am a great devotee of your poetry." She smiled up at him and he realized she barely came to his shoulder. "I dabble a wee bit, though I'm quite willing to become a student of yours."

He said nothing, adjusting to the fact he was suddenly being pursued. More than one London miss vied for his affections over the years but he'd grown especially adept at remaining guarded. Politely aloof. Something told him that between Charis and Miss Lyon he was going to be less successful in future.

He met her eyes. "You subscribe to *Tatler*, I take it."

"*The Female Spectator*, too, as well as *The Scots Magazine*. But I'm most partial to *The Queen Bee Chronicles: A Georgian Gazette for Elegance and Enlightenment*."

A well-read lass, then? "I've not heard of the latter."

"Oh? 'Tis fairly new and all the rage among the literary set, at least the ladies. The founder is rumored to be a Scotswoman."

A Scotswoman with considerable financial resources, he didn't say as they sought the punch bowl. Founding a magazine was a lofty literary achievement, especially for a female. As a poet with no annual stipend from the Crown and the last son of an earl, he'd never realized that ambition. Not yet.

"Nae doubt the mystery of its founder lends to wider circulation," he jested.

"You sound rather jaded, sir." She laughed. "Or are you jealous?"

"Mayhap both," he admitted with a smile. "Often periodicals are short lived but I wish it every success if only for your enjoyment."

She extended a lace fan and waved it about in the heated air. "Your niece is having a splendid debut. When is the following function?"

"Dunhaven Keep hosts a fête Saturday next."

"Then we shall meet again," she said, looking up at him, intention in her gaze.

11

The reading of the will left a bitter taste in Maryn's mouth. If Grandfather had only consulted her about the matter first. Warned her of leaving Nicola out of it to a large degree.

"I'm astonished," Nicola told the Edinburgh solicitors in the library's dark confines. "A meagre five thousand pounds is not what I had in mind. Are you certain you're not overlooking anything?"

Unfortunately, the lead solicitor seemed to have taken an instant dislike to Nicola from the moment they'd met. Maryn stayed quiet, letting them have their say. What could she possibly add given she'd inherited nearly everything?

"Five thousand pounds is no small sum," he replied, frowning. "You are the youngest in the family and, as such, are fortunate to receive what your late grandfather so generously provided."

"If I were a man I'd contest it," she replied, looking at Lord Marchmont as if expecting him to intervene.

But the peely-wally Lord M, as Maryn had begun to think of him, simply met his wife's stare with bleary eyes. Was Nicola worried he might die and she'd be left destitute? Maryn had no idea the state of their financial affairs. When the solicitors had left, Maryn turned to her sister in concern.

"If you are in need of funds—"

"Fortunate for you to say." Nicola stood, her fury a fiery mask. "I find it ghastly that you, as Herschel's twin, have inherited the entirety of Grandfather's estate. Never for one moment shall I forget it is rightfully our brother's."

"Nor shall I," Maryn replied at once.

"A double travesty given you are likely to never marry and so our family line will end, thus we are in danger of forfeiting everything."

That sad possibility needed no pointing out. Maryn looked at the library clock, wishing them on their way.

Nicola continued hotly, "If our situations were reversed I could at least have bequeathed the estate to my heirs and the son we soon hope to have."

How could she have forgotten? Maryn looked to Nicola's waist, her throat so tight she couldn't offer congratulations.

Nicola pulled on her gloves. "Perhaps you will be so inclined as to rightfully reward us when you come to your senses about matters. My greatest hope is that our son will inherit the duchy one day."

Stung by embarrassment, Maryn said nothing. 'Twas one thing to muse on such a matter privately but to express it in such a blatantly ill-mannered way? And with such blistering blame as if she'd all but killed Herschel then stolen his inheritance to boot. All benevolent thoughts flew out of Maryn's head. She could only hope her three nieces would be nothing like their entitled mother.

The offended couple swept out though Lord M cast her what seemed a slightly apologetic look as he did so. Maryn's hopes that they would have harmoniously brought their daughters and tarried for a meal or even spent the night were dashed. They hadn't brought the girls, they'd only stayed for the reading of the will, and had shunned her invitation. Maryn had heard some women suffered from nerves when *enceinte* as the French said. Perhaps, in her condition, Nicola was the same?

She left the library, glad to find Rosemary in the hall. Her smile was a balm for the fractious forenoon. "Such a bonny day. Pure sunshine and nae wind. Would you like yer dinner in the garden, Your Grace?"

"A lovely idea, thank you. I'll be in Grandfather's cabinet till then."

Rosemary whispered, "*Yer* cabinet."

"Ah, so it is." Maryn smiled past her soreness. "I haven't quite gotten used to the idea that he's away permanently and I'm now completely here."

"D'ye miss the cottage?"

"Sometimes I'm tempted to return to it. I miss Bassett and Jamesina. The simplicity of a few rooms. The orangery. All the birds and wild creatures. How about you?"

"Nay." She pursed her lips as a footman passed by. "I'd be fey to choose a cottage o'er a castle. Folk would talk and I'm jealous of yer reputation."

Folks do love to talk, Maryn didn't say.

"Time t' reverse the Lockhart curse, if ye dinna mind my saying so."

Maryn almost laughed despite herself. "One of your best attributes is your honesty, Rosemary. Glad I am of it."

Flushing, the maid gave a seamless curtsey which she'd obviously been practicing. "I promise t' ne'er give ye cause to doubt me. I rather enjoy being a lady's maid."

"Are your new garments coming soon from the dressmaker?"

"Och! Tomorrow she'll be here with the finished gowns and underpinnings. I canna thank ye enough!" Beaming, she excused herself and went upstairs to resume doing whatever lady's maids did.

It was hard to remain melancholy in Rosemary's perpetually cheerful presence. She was all sunshine whereas Nicola was a dreich day. Wanting to shake off their morning meeting, Maryn returned to her cabinet. Fresh-cut roses filled a four foot tall porcelain Chinese vase atop a side table, perfuming the chamber. She'd not changed anything in this sumptuous room yet. Might she begin by replacing the painting over the mantel? Grandmother, regal as she was, belonged in the Portrait Gallery, not here looking down on her rather mournful granddaughter as if admonishing her. For Maryn felt thoroughly admonished of late.

Try as she might, she seemed to be a disaster at estate management. Such bored her to tears. Her passion was words, period. But lately even words failed her, on paper especially. Her new responsibilities left no time for her usual creative pursuits. She hadn't even time to peruse the circulation numbers of *The Queen Bee Chronicles*. Nor savor the satisfaction she'd founded it the year before.

All was business and ledgers, a dreadful thing she had no head for. An estate manager was in order as the former had died shortly before Grandfather. But where was she to start looking for one?

She couldn't consult Everard Hume, known far beyond Berwickshire borders for his landowning prowess, including those in his employ. Reliable, honest stewards and managers were hard to come by. Straightening the stack of ledgers, she grabbed hold of a consoling thought. She would ask Lord Stair his recommendation ...

She took out a list of all the duchy's tenants, many whose names she recognized. Grandfather had been a generous, conscientious laird as Mrs. Duncan had said. Maryn wouldn't change that though the estate had changed hands. Sending an unspoken plea heavenward, she fought the inclination to read another of Orin's letters.

"Your Grace ... " The housekeeper appeared in the doorway, ever helpful and perhaps heavensent. "I thought I might offer you some counsel given you asked me to bring you the house-hold account books yesterday."

"Please come in." Maryn brightened. "I was just mulling the matter rather unsatisfactorily. I'm unsure where to start."

"Inheriting an estate of this size must be overwhelming and with the estate manager's untimely passing, God rest him, a finer man cannot be had." She sat opposite Maryn and pulled spectacles from her pocket. "If it's any consolation, I worked closely with the late Mr. McCullough for many years, especially when his eyesight began to fail."

"I had no idea."

"He was loathe to tell your ailing grandfather and so we just continued on as best we could. The estate itself, largely due to McCullough, always turned a profit. Half of the land lies fallow and all the tenants are in good standing, nary a one in arrears. But there are always needs to be met."

"Such as?"

"Your grandfather insisted on a month-by-month report of each family on Lockhart lands. McCullough and I would go out together to make the rounds and visit each dwelling, determine a course of action and so forth. That hasn't been done since he passed and your grandfather began failing."

Maryn grew concerned. Tenants were an ongoing responsibility though she'd never been privy to this sort of business. Surely she wasn't expected to visit them herself given both her disfigurement and sad history seemed a magnet for gawking. She shuddered at the thought. "What do you recommend in Mr. McCullough's absence, then?"

"Hutchins is senior footman and has been at the Hall the longest. He has a head for business and is on good footing with most of the tenants given McCullough often used him as liaison. I'd suggest sending Hutchins and myself to make the rounds. Perhaps he'd even make a competent steward in time."

"Would he be amenable to that?"

"I canna speak for him, of course, but he is faithful and trustworthy and able-bodied. Being midlife and unmarried, he is wholly invested here."

"I shall consider it then, thank you. Go ahead and make the rounds again then report to me like you did Grandfather. How long has it been since you've gone about the estate?"

"Last March, Your Grace."

"Overdue, then. I'll look forward to hearing what has transpired since spring."

Mrs. Duncan looked relieved. "We shall forge ahead with your blessing. I do ken a fever and a difficult birth among the tenants. There are always concerns and demands given the sizable number of them."

"Of course. Since Grandfather was often away, I'm beginning to sense you and Mr. McCullough managed here very adeptly." Maryn regarded her thoughtfully. "Which merits an increase in wages, surely."

"Weel, I couldna—"

"Please, Mrs. Duncan, I'm sure my late grandfather would agree. Consider it your duty." Maryn smiled, feeling a lift in her own spirits. "And convey the same to Hutchins, please."

12

*O*rin took a saddled Septimus from the stables, past the arched west gate and mile-long drive onto the Merse. He skirted a spruce wood to gain open parkland and then Langton Burn, a winding stream near the burial place of a medieval Hume. Here he halted, looking down at the pile of stone atop a fallen warrior of long ago. A reminder of Fast Castle, another ancient relic that hugged the coast. An oft repeated couplet from boyhood came to mind.

Fastcastle, firm and sure,
On the rock will aye endure.

It belonged to the Humes still, a shattered hulk battered by incessant winds that threatened to topple what little remained into the North Sea. Once he'd fancied restoring it but the laird had laughed heartily and called him daft. A dreamer. He was certainly guilty of the latter.

He rode toward the sea, past tenants bringing home dried peats or laboring in the fields amid grazing livestock. He breathed in a dozen earthy scents, moor grass and Lady's-mantle rising to his horse's flanks. He nearly trespassed on Lockhart land. Midsummer was at hand, the stuff of poetry and legend and ... romance.

No sooner had he thought it than a figure on horseback appeared and headed straight toward him. Ivory Lyon? Aye, followed by what seemed to be a groom. It took only a trice to see what an expert horsewoman she was. Spying Orin, she spurred on her sleek chestnut mare all the faster.

"Mr. Hume." Undisguised delight shone in her eyes. "Fancy meeting you across this wide expanse of Merse."

"The bonny day seems to call for it," he said, squinting in the sunlight.

"Where are you headed?"

"Nowhere in particular. And you?"

"The same. Perhaps we shall ramble together."

He eyed the groom, a Duns lad he remembered who swore like a coachman. Orin's desire to ride alone dissolved like the moor's mist as they took off at a canter east, the groom trailing.

"You've a fine mount bred for the hunt, I take it." He wouldn't say he couldn't stand the sport. Chasing down the Almighty's most vulnerable creatures was not something he stomached.

"Papa hunts his hounds four days a week from November to March." She looked about as if getting her bearings. "I get quite worn out, though I do relish a good race now and again. Shall we?"

Was she … challenging him?

They had unwittingly come near the site he avoided. He'd not been here for years, not since the accident. Distracted by her company he'd nearly ridden right up to it. Summer's verdancy was in no way similar to the bite of a blizzard that long ago day but her playful words were the same.

Shall we?

The dare echoed in his ears, switching from her high lilt to Herschel's wind-battered shout. In a trice the landscape shifted. Orin felt transported with such force he grew lightheaded as the sun faded and winter rushed in. The chill that hit him was akin to a snow-sharded wind.

Shall we? Shall we? Shall we?

And then came the sickening thud of colliding sleighs. Screaming. No one was where they should have been, neither horses or humans. All was bloody madness—

"I dare you!" Miss Lyon had slowed and spun round beneath the tree that bore the brunt of Herschel's collision.

Orin stared past her to the Birnam oak, the fissured bark still bearing telltale scars. The tree had recovered far better than he. Better than Maryn. It had taken Herschel's life. The horror was etched deep in his being but he knew for Maryn and family it was far worse. They had lost a beloved brother—the heir to a duchy—

"Mr. Hume?" Miss Lyon approached, near enough to place a gloved hand on his arm.

Her gentle touch grounded him but he still felt choked. Frozen. Mired in the moment. Forcing his gaze from the tree, he fastened it instead on a carriage coming down the distant road. With its large wheels and ducal coat of arms, Orin knew it immediately. Not the Lowland dukes of Buccleuch or Roxburghe or Montrose.

Fordyce.

Maryn sat back in the coach, hardly aware of the landscape unfolding around her so caught up was she in the details of the day's visits. To her astonishment she didn't even feel queasy from the coach ride. Elated was the better word. Uplifted.

And he that watereth shall be watered also himself.

Shortly after dawn, one and thirty baskets had been loaded atop the coach, filled with an assortment of goods for the first round of tenant families, including sewing and knitting supplies, tea, toys, tobacco and foodstuffs, to name but a few. Alas, Mrs. Duncan had fallen ill the night before and there was no postponement, thus Maryn went in her place, Rosemary with her. The steward-in-training, Hutchins, rode postilion.

Summoning every shred of courage she had, and disguising her disfigurement as best she could, she said a prayer and sallied forth. She, who had hidden in a cottage for years, was being forced into the open like a hothouse flower. How she chafed at this new role. But determination to get off on the right foot with Grandfather's tenants came first.

The first cottage they came to held an old, blind woman cared for by her daughter, a spinner, and her crippled yeoman husband. The next held newborn triplets, a very weakened mother, and a father injured in a milling accident. Other tenants were less needy and more independent, but all seemed glad to get baskets of goods and a visit from the new duchess herself.

Quickly she forgot herself and her small infirmities, attuned to the needs around her. A wet nurse must be gotten to help feed the triplets, a doctor for the infirm, new roofing and windows for cottages damaged by a recent storm, and some means of education for the growing number of children needing to be schooled.

None of the adults had any books save a rare Bible. Few could read nor had the time, given they labored from sunup to sundown. Therefore the learning must start young while the children still had the hours and inclination. But how to begin?

At the end of the visits she'd momentarily lost sight of her fears, her need to stay hidden, as she faced those far less fortunate, at least materially. And her desire to help had her recording their names and needs in the ledger she'd brought lest she forget.

"Will ye return to us, Yer Grace?" one woman said. "Ye bring us a bit o' cheer, just like yer dear mother once did, God rest her."

"My wife seems better for yer company," the husband of another told her. "And dearly needs yer remedy ye brought."

But it was the barefoot bairns with their soiled, searching faces who knew no better than to tug on her skirts for attention that most wrenched her heart. She still felt their wee fingers examining the rich folds of her petticoats as they gaped astonished at her buckled shoes and befeathered hat. Had she dressed too lavishly? That had not been her intent. None seemed to notice her injury though she was careful to disguise what she could with a glove.

She pondered the wee ones now, forgetting what she did. Forgetting to turn her face away from the dreadful site till it was too late. The open carriage window faced meadowland that was not white and frigid but green and sun-warmed. Yet still the past rushed back. The massive tree—the icy curve of land that lent to the speed of the sleighs—

Revulsion grabbed her by the throat, so strong and sudden she struggled to breathe. Yet she couldn't look away—couldn't remove herself from the scene. Her horror at happening by unawares was eclipsed only by her shock at seeing the familiar figure on the hill.

She would ken Orin Hume anywhere, no matter the passage of time. Only he wasn't alone on horseback. A lady was alongside, the both of them at a standstill facing the road Maryn's coach trundled down as it raised a storm of gritty brown dust.

She froze, eyes on the man she hadn't seen in years. A stone's throw away, he was staring straight at her. An expert horseman, he looked especially fine astride a black stallion. A green wool frock coat caught her eye but he was hatless—he'd ever been hatless while riding—his dark blonde hair tied behind. The rest of him blurred and she pressed her spine against the velvet upholstered seat as if to shrink from sight.

"Are ye all right?" Rosemary regarded her with wide-eyed alarm as they continued on at a pace far too slow to suit Maryn.

Maryn coughed and her maid closed the window curtain
to block the dust. A dozen possibilities turned her mind into a
spinning top. Orin here. Orin home. Orin possibly wed with
his wife riding alongside him. The stalwart image of him—even
more braw than she remembered—would never leave her, nearly
as distressing as the site itself.

Once home, she disappeared into Grandfather's cabinet and
shut the door. Trying to collect herself, she paced the chamber,
feeling caged within its blue-damask walls. She wanted nothing
more than to return to the Merse and run toward the man she'd
once known and fling herself into his arms. She wanted to be the
untried lass she'd once been. She wanted him to be the lad she'd
loved, untouched by tragedy and time. A swelling anguish rose
inside her till she felt half-suffocated.

Unable to stand it any longer, she unlocked the letters from
the secret drawer with a trembling hand and all but tore the
second one open. But it was hardly what she expected.

Dear Maryn,

    Though we are far apart the bond between us remains unbro-
ken. A threefold cord. I pray fervently for your health and happi-
ness, and write this humble poem with you in mind.

    Round the tree of life the flowers
    Are ranged, abundant, even;
    Its crest on every side spreads out
    On the fields and plains of Heaven.
    Glorious flocks of singing birds
    Celebrate their truth,
    Green abounding branches bear
    Choicest leaves and fruit.
    The lovely flocks maintain their song
    In the changeless weather

A hundred feathers for every bird,
A hundred tunes for every feather.

> *Your entire,*
> *Orin Hume*

Had he been reminding her of the eternal? That Herschel, with his heart for holy things, was in heaven? And the birds … she and Herschel had shared a love of befeathered creatures. Surely the poet in him had that in mind.

It cut her to the quick, this simple bit of verse. Tears spattered the paper and she lay it aside, digging for a handkerchief in her pocket. If she'd read this when he'd sent it, might it have helped her? Assuaged her somehow? Now, so long after, she could only wonder why Grandfather had withheld it from her.

How fine Orin had looked along that lonesome stretch of ground. And how very companionable with that fashionably dressed lady beside him.

He had clearly moved on though she had not.

13

$\mathcal{A}$nother function, this time at Lyon Court. With Charis on his arm and Lord Lovell on hand it went better than expected. Orin hoped it would help distract him from what had happened on the Merse. But even the glitter and hubbub of the ballroom didn't put a dent in the memory of the Fordyce coach coming by unexpectedly, the last conveyance he'd expected to see on the road, and certainly the last duchess.

He'd not gotten a good look at Maryn at the funeral, clad head to toe in black as she'd been, but he had locked eyes with her for just a trice day before yesterday, the coach window framing her. That fleeting look cost him what little peace he had over the situation. Not peace, exactly, but resignation. He'd finally resigned himself to not hearing from her, not being a part of her life.

Till he'd seen her again.

"Mr. Hume." A brusque voice wrenched him from his musings as he stood in an alcove by open French doors. "I've been wanting to speak to you and perhaps now is the time."

Turning, he greeted Lord Lyon who bore an uncanny resemblance to his daughter, his Glaswegian speech distinct.

"Ivory speaks well of you. Being somewhat new to Berwickshire I'm slowly becoming aware of the locals as it were."

"I'm well acquainted with your Kerrs," Orin replied. "Since Border Reiver days."

"Ah, yes, thank heavens we've moved to more civilized times and only need contend with the Jacobite threat." He chuckled and took a drink from the glass he carried. "My daughter tells me you are often at Court in London and seldom here."

"That may change in future."

"England is a far cry from Scotland. I'm surprised you're so far afield." He eyed Orin with open respect. "Poet Laureate, nae less."

How lofty he made it sound when the reality was quite different. "As the seventh son of a Lowland laird, there's not much left to do but go rhyming and collect the tierce of wine that comes with it."

"The seventh son! By jove, I hope to have as many grandsons one day. I've quite given up on an heir after three daughters, Ivory being the firstborn and of marriageable age."

Orin weathered the man's bluntness. He was used to meddlesome mothers but meddlesome fathers?

"We hope to see you more at Lyon Court in future. A fox hunt, perhaps, in the fall."

"I dinna hunt though your daughter tells me she accompanies you."

The man looked affronted. "A shame, Hume, but truly, no finer lass to be had in the field. She's safely apart from any danger but is quite fond of the hounds and usually wins the brush."

Orin almost smiled, imagining the lovely Miss Lyon claiming a fox's tail at hunt's end.

Lord Lyon continued. "Perhaps we could convince you to attend a hunt ball, at least."

"I may be away later this year. A prior commitment."

"Ah, the king's Birthnight Ball, I suppose." He took another drink. "I'll read about it after, I'm sure. The papers will trumpet such about as usual."

Orin stifled a yawn. Had he sufficiently deterred Lord Lyon from thinking him a serious suitor? Who would want a son-in-law who could claim but a tierce of wine and the haphazard sale of his literary endeavors as his bride price?

"I recently heard you've been awarded a baronetcy from the Crown."

Meaning my niece has been telling fairy tales, he almost replied. In truth, the king, likely sensing his disenchantment, offered him the title before he'd last left London. "I declined it."

Astonishment washed Lord Lyon's face. Before the man could ask for clarification, Miss Lyon appeared.

"There you are, the both of you." Searchingly, she looked from her father to Orin as if trying to guess the gist of their conversation. "The minuet has finally ended and the country dances are about to begin. I was hoping..."

She said it so sweetly, so beseechingly, that Orin was moved to answer. "Allow me, then."

Maryn replaced the third and fourth of Orin's opened letters in the desk's locked compartment. One line lingered in her thoughts.

I retain an unalterable affection for you, which neither time or distance can change.

Two letters remained to be read. Each extracted a heavy price from her. She was now torn between telling Orin about Grandfather's actions if only to explain away her lack of response.

Or should she just let matters alone?

She needed time to think and there was no better place to think than the privacy of Thistle Cottage.

Orin could wait no longer. Rising early after the Lyon Court ball, he took a walk in Wedderburn's formal garden to clear his head and decide once and for all. Five years separation wasn't an age but given the circumstances, it seemed so. And his own future seemed to demand he do something. He'd decided a great many things in the month he'd been home and Maryn was a part of it.

"Uncle Orin, why are you awake so early?"

He looked up and saw a yawning Charis leaning from her bedchamber window on the second floor.

"Why aren't you?" he shot back.

"All this birdsong is like kirk bells pealing! I'd have to be in a windowless room to avoid it."

"I try never to avoid it." He took a bench, back to her, facing the Merse. "'Tis nine of the clock, sleepyhead. The best hours are in the morn."

Her answer was to slam the shutters closed but even that wouldn't keep the symphony out. He focused on one lark in particular, singing its delicate song on the wing as it rose over the wisteria arbor and vanished from sight. Mist was rising in every direction, hazing the route he'd soon take.

If he dared.

Should he seek his brother's counsel before riding out? The laird was a very practical man. Suppose Everard tried to dissuade him? *Let sleeping dogs lie*, he could almost hear him say. It wasn't the answer Orin wanted. And in truth, what mattered most was the Almighty's opinion. Only he hadn't asked Him either.

Or mayhap the Almighty had put the idea in his head to begin with.

Spurred on by the thought, he went to the stables and took time saddling Septimus himself in place of a groom. Doing so gave him more time to reconsider all the fine points and possible ramifications of what he was about to do.

Another half hour hadn't deterred him so he set out, measuring the distance between Wedderburn Castle and Lockhart Hall by markers he remembered and some that were new to him. An old dyke. A handsome stone house behind newly raised iron gates. A marshy stretch of ground where waterfowl flocked. The road here was less traveled as it wound beyond the heart of Berwickshire, the landscape lonesome save the sheep grazing on gently folding hills.

Once one of the leading families of the Lowlands, the Lockharts had lost their place. Little was known since Herschel passed and even the demise of the duke had been a quiet affair. What had happened at the reading of the will? Who had inherited the duchy?

Heaven forbid Lady Maryn think his visit based on prying.

He raised a leather glove and dashed away the sweat beading his brow. The summer sun blinded him as he passed beyond gates he'd suspected might be closed. Stately lime trees along the drive were in full flower, their canopy humming with bees and winged insects.

He'd always revered Lockhart Hall's history. Built centuries ago, its royal roots gave it a special polish and pedigree. A newer wing with a round room at one end was the former duke's doing but he liked the medieval hall best, much as he liked old Wedderburn best.

No sign of life enlivened the place. His spirits, stalwart till now, began to sink. Had the house been shuttered, the servants dispersed?

He dismounted near the carriage block, tethering Septimus to an iron rail. His heart seemed as heavy as his tread upon the front entrance steps. The bronze unicorn door knocker with its French phrasing almost made him smile. He'd been fascinated by it as a child. *Dieu et mon droit, God and my right,* a motto on the British royal arms which mirrored the Lockhart's tie.

He struck the weathered plate and waited. Five seconds. Ten. It was early. Too early, mayhap. A sudden wind rifled his queued hair as he removed his new hat—which Charis had declared fine enough for courting—and tucked it beneath one arm. All the carefully thought-out words he'd been prepared to say were fast becoming a sinking stew.

Should he leave? Admit defeat?

His step back seemed to swing the front door open. A middle-aged footman stared at him with no small surprise. "G'morning, sir."

Nae retreat.

"I've come to see Lady Maryn." Orin darted a look at the central stair over the servant's liveried shoulder. "Is she at home?"

The footman seemed strangely flummoxed. "Do come in, sir."

Orin stepped into the cool, tiled hall, similar to Wedderburn's. The footman disappeared, leaving him to take in a house mostly unchanged, at least to his memory.

"Mr. Hume?" A female voice held familiarity. "Can it be?"

He faced a tiny woman in an enormous mobcap and apron. "Mrs. Duncan?"

"Indeed." She smiled up at him, every inch the kind, capable soul he recalled. "I'm still here, sir, and doubtless always will be."

"Glad I am of it. I'd begun to wonder if anyone was home."

"Och, so many changes of late." She gave a little sigh. "Hutchins says you're seeking Her Grace."

Orin was hard pressed to hide his surprise. The *duchess*?

Mrs. Duncan looked over his shoulder to the front door that hadn't been shut. "That would be her leaving."

He turned to see the dust he'd raised rise again. A chaise was barely visible. "When will she return?"

"She didna say, sir." Suddenly Mrs. Duncan looked as disappointed as the footman had been flummoxed. "But when she does I shall surely tell her you called."

He nodded. "If this was London I'd leave my card but here it seems out of place."

"I do believe 'tis appreciated even here in the Borders." She smiled, revealing a missing tooth. "'Tis not every day one receives the Poet Laureate of Britain."

So, she knew about that? Not many servants were lettered. He took the engraved ivory card from his pocket and handed it to her. It bore his name. Not his status. Nor the ludicrous baronetcy Lyon had mentioned.

He thanked her and turned away with a sense of urgency, ready to ride and catch up with Maryn if he could. But by the time he'd traversed the long lime avenue the dust had settled and all his hopes with it.

The newly titled Duchess of Fordyce was nowhere in sight.

14

Thistle Cottage was blessedly quiet. Just what Maryn hoped for. While Rosemary put the kettle on for tea, Maryn went into the garden, Orin's remaining letters tucked in her pocket. She'd memorized the poem he'd written her, the last lines especially.

The lovely flocks maintain their song
In the changeless weather
A hundred feathers for every bird,
A hundred tunes for every feather.

For a time she just sat, birdsong all about her. Her injury was ailing her, as unpredictable as a weathervane. The bone-deep ache promised a storm of some sort. Since it was midsummer it would likely be wind and rain. She looked down at her arm, the gloved hand disguising the twisted fingers. Once she'd been repulsed. Now it simply made her sad. She felt like an injured bird, her wing broken.

With her good hand, she pulled an unopened letter from her pocket, broke the seal with a swipe of her finger, and smoothed the paper out on her lap. While these missives didn't qualify as love letters, the familiar sloping of Orin's Copperplate script still made her insides swirl. Correspondence from her publishing contacts hadn't quite the same appeal.

Dear Maryn,

Since I have not yet heard from you, my mind would silence my heart and leave off writing again. But the heart wins. It has won for years now. There has never been anyone else who came first in my affections but you.

Not heard from her? With a sickening realization she returned to his opening words. Her heart seemed to stop. He'd kept writing to her even when he had no answer? What had happened to all her letters to him? Long, impassioned letters that made her blush even to recall them now.

She read on hungrily—heartbreakingly.

And so when our families began marriage negotiations—such a cold term for so fine a feeling—it seemed natural. Expected. And more than welcome. But life as we know it has a way of testing even the finest things. In this case, a loss we could never have imagined. Mayhap I am too bold to suggest that we hold onto what we have—or had—before the tragedy. I, for one, have not changed in regards to you. My love for you is steadfast and enduring, surely the stuff of what the best marriages are made. But of course, two must make a marriage, and your consent or the lack of it now that the period of mourning is over, determines our future direction.

My highest hope is that I will hear from you. But if not, I will respectfully take your silence as your answer.

Your entire,
Orin Hume

Her heart, so sore at even the best of times, threatened to burst. She looked toward Wedderburn Castle, trying to reconcile the present with the past. So, he'd once cared for her, enough to marry her.

Then who was that young woman she'd seen him riding with upon the very ground of the accident? Had he told her the dire events of that day? Perhaps he'd come to terms with what had happened and didn't shun the place like she did.

She refolded the letter, wishing she could do the same with her feelings. Warm, effusive feelings that had no further place in her heart. Though she wished Grandfather had given her the letters, would she have done anything differently if he had?

The facts remained and trumped any fine feeling. She was part invalid. She could not do her own hair, could not dress without help. She could no longer ride a horse nor play the pianoforte nor dance nor do anything that required two whole hands. She could not even pick up a child, at least safely. Her injury oft pained her, more emotionally than physically.

Did that not exclude her from marriage?

She let the last letter stay in her pocket. She was not ready to read it nor reckon with its contents. For the moment she simply wanted to sit here in the sunlight and breathe in the floral fragrance carried on the wind.

Orin, recently returned from Lockhart Hall and a long, hard ride on the Merse, came in a few minutes late with little thought as to the dinner hour. The hall clock reminded him and so, after washing up in an antechamber, he joined the countess in the smaller parlor she preferred instead of the dining room. Dinner was just the two of them. Charis had gone to Duns with Lord Lovell and a groom while the laird had been called away to a meeting at kirk.

"I'm glad you're continuing to take meals with us," Blythe told him as a footman served them. "Life in the gatehouse isn't too solitary, I hope."

"Solitude is a sublime concept, lonesomeness an altogether different animal."

Her eyes registered understanding. "You're lonely, then."

"The gatehouse is ideal but should be shared."

"I'm glad to hear it. I never imagined you a lifelong bachelor. Given you're the age Everard was when he wed me, you are still young."

"Two and thirty is not auld, aye, and seems to turn a man's mind to domestic matters."

"I can see you with a wife and children. But somehow I cannot see you with any of the misses this social season."

"Nor can I." A dozen feminine faces flashed through his mind. "I don't want a titled and ornamented mannequin but a wife."

"Some seem quite... vacuous." She chose her words carefully, clearly reluctant to criticize. "Charis told me she introduced you to Miss Lyon."

"But..." He took a drink of claret and waited for her answer.

"That is for you to decide, not me. I tend to forget I'm not your mother though I was cast in that role once upon a time."

"For which I'm grateful. You came into our lives when sorely needed." He meant it wholeheartedly. His memories of his mother were hazy and his father little better. "And I believe you broke the mold. There are few learned women like you who have a passion for the written word."

"Being fluent in Greek and Hebrew made me rather peculiar years ago though your brother wasn't deterred. As for you, I do feel a woman who shares your literary pursuits would be most welcome. One that supports them, at least."

"I agree with you. But where is she?"

The question seemed laughable. *She* was eight miles away. Where else? But Blythe was too kind to mention it. They dined in companionable quiet a few minutes, Orin's thoughts on his morning's failed mission, not his full plate.

When he could stand it no longer, he said, "I've been to Lockhart Hall."

Blythe paused, fork suspended. "To see Lady Maryn."

"She wasn't at home and is now the duchess."

"Oh my ... the plot thickens very much upon us."

"Very much, aye. I left my card and spoke with their longtime housekeeper."

"Will you return?"

"I'm now wondering why I went in the first place."

"Why did you?" she asked gently.

"You recall we were in the midst of a marriage settlement between Maryn and myself when the tragedy happened."

"What I most remember is how dismayed—nay, devastated—we were when all came to an abrupt halt. We looked forward to welcoming her as your bride. The late duke was as desirous to see the union happen as we were. And then ... "

"I believe that needs to be addressed again."

Sadness gave way to astonishment. "You would ask for her hand—after all that has happened?"

Orin took another bracing drink of wine. "Call me an idiot but I feel an obligation to her—nay, that's not the right word. More a matter of honor, if a complicated one."

"Matters of honor often are. 'Tis bold, even brave."

"I doubt the laird would see it in the same light."

"But the laird is not here and this is not his choice. I respect my husband's counsel though he's been accused of being rather jaded at times. Decidedly not of a romantic nature except," she amended with a slight smile, "when it comes to me."

"I am the unquestionable romantic in the clan." How often he'd wished otherwise. To be like his soldierly brother had been his dream since childhood. But he and Everard couldn't be more different.

"Do you still care for her?"

He stilled.

When I saw her again my heart turned over in such a rush it seemed to have all but ground to a halt in her absence. My very soul seemed to shout though I had no words. My love for her is boundless. It defies time. Distance. Sorrow. There is something of the eternal in it.

He simply said, "I've cared for Maryn for so long, long before I even realized there was substance to it. I will always care for her. Mayhap that's why I can't let this rest now."

Blythe regarded him in silence for a few moments. "So, you are willing to go ahead with marrying her if she agrees as she once did. Or if she refuses, to release you, so to speak from your prior commitment, and give you liberty to move on."

"That's the gist of it. A fool's errand, mayhap, given our current circumstances." He could already hear the critics lambast the situation. "Why would a duchess dabble with a poet?"

"I, for one, think that a silly argument. If she still loves you such is moot."

"She never responded to my letters. Let that be my answer, some would say."

"*Some* will always say and think the worst. Give them not the slightest notice."

They grew quiet as a footman whisked their empty plates away. Dessert was served—some sort of flummery—but they just sat without indulging.

"Much to ponder and pray about then," Lady Blythe said, lifting a spoon.

Despite the gravity of the subject, the regrettable past and the unknown future, Orin looked at her with thanks. Even if nothing had been decided or resolved, he was glad he'd come home to the Lowlands.

15

"Mr. Hume was here?" Maryn took the finely-engraved card from Mrs. Duncan, her mouth dropping open like a drawbridge. "In this very hall?"

"Indeed he was, Your Grace." The housekeeper seemed as pleased as she was surprised. "And such a celebrated Hume. The brawest of the bunch!"

"Certainly the most literary," Maryn remarked, passing into her cabinet. Today the round room was grey, reflecting the storm her bones had predicted. Such weather would surely keep him from visiting again. She was safe for now, at least.

Safe. Safe from his intentions or her own fractured feelings?

Heart in her throat, she asked, "Did he say he would return?"

"He did not," Mrs. Duncan said flatly, her disappointment plain.

"I can't imagine why he'd call. There was no one else with him?" The lass he'd been with along the road wouldn't budge in her mind, flawless as she was.

"Nary a soul."

Maryn slowly lowered to the settee facing the hearth's low fire. She'd just escaped the rain but the chill seemed to have followed her. For the moment it felt like winter again.

"Tea is needed, and your mother's best Sêvres porcelain." Mrs. Duncan hastened away, surely in need of a dish herself.

Maryn removed her right glove and looked to the card in her lap. So, he'd come. After long years and unanswered letters later.

Why?

She brought the paper to her nose and sighed aloud at the unmistakable hint of clary sage and citrus. He had not changed one whit in that regard. And her fleeting look at him on the Merse told her he'd grown more stalwart man and less the lanky lad she remembered.

But again, what did it matter? She'd best take care lest her imagination spin him into some sort of romanticized, faux figure she'd lose her heart and soul to all over again.

"Here you are, Your Grace." Mrs. Duncan set down the tray. "Cook has baked the chocolate biscuits you're so fond of and I've brewed Bohea."

Despite Orin, Maryn felt a sudden contentment in such small blessings as confections and lovely cups. He preferred coffee, she recalled. With a hefty dash of cream and sugar. She'd given him a coffee-mill once. Did he still have it?

As she drank tea and ate biscuits on a decidedly uneasy stomach she was left alone to ponder his visit. She would not, of course, return it by going to Wedderburn Castle. Perish the thought! Instead, she considered reading his final letter, as of yet still sealed. But the anticipation of it—comingled with dread— kept her from opening it. Feelings were ever fickle and she felt on a seesaw of them. She had gone to the cottage in the nick of time thus avoiding his unexpected arrival.

Or had it been the most unfortunate, untimely absence in her life?

"Are you ready, Uncle?" Charis appeared at the stable's entrance, a vision in violet.

Lovell certainly thought so, staring down at her with an awestruck air. Observing them, Orin felt that odd emptiness take hold. Would he ever again experience the flush of first love? He well recalled what it had been like. Passion—some would say infatuation—left a somewhat confident man feeling a bumbling, tongue-tied fool. In the best of ways.

"Ready," he finally answered from atop Septimus.

They were joining up with a party to ride to the ruins of Hume Castle, one of the best vantage points on the Merse. He'd been appointed resident tour guide based on his knowledge of Hume history. They were conveniently riding by Lyon Court where Miss Lyon lived who, Charis told him, was keen to learn Borders history, too.

Soon they were passing vestiges of ancient cairns and standing stones to gain the rocky outcrop and the crumbling walls of Hume Castle with its commanding views.

"Once this was one of the most formidable strongholds in the Borders," Orin told them. "A rarity built with a rectangular courtyard after Highland fortresses. The Humes were wardens of the Merse, guarding Scottish territory." He pointed toward the long-disputed boundary in the distance. "Only five miles from here lies England who fought us for centuries over control of this country."

"They were among the fighting clans who rode as Reivers by moonlight," Miss Lyon added. "Including my Kerrs."

He nodded. "Hard to believe there's just a warm wind and endless sheep today when once there was the clash of conflict everywhere."

"Frightful and dangerous," Miss Lyon said with a shudder as she dismounted.

They settled on the grounds for refreshments carried by two footmen and overseen by Charis herself. She smiled at him as he sat and leaned back against the castle's sun-warmed wall. "What is this moveable feast called, Uncle Orin? I do believe you poets have a name for it. This was your idea after all."

"*Pique nique*," he answered in French. "From a satirical seventeenth-century poem about a priest known for visiting friends armed with bottles and dishes."

They laughed as the servants distributed veal and ham pies, cheese, cucumbers, fresh fruit, and more biscuits, butter, and beverages than their party of ten could possibly hold.

"Mother told me not to overpack but you men are always ravenous," Charis said, sitting down beside Lovell on a blanket. "I grew up with five brothers and I've not forgotten."

"So…" Miss Lyon turned to Orin as side conversations ensued all around them. "Would you like lemonade or ginger-beer?"

"The latter," Orin said, as a footman poured him a full glass.

"A delightful idea you had with this." She tasted a ripe strawberry. "I'm starting to feel more insider than outsider after spending time with you Merse-men and women. You're quite hospitable on the whole."

"Some of us more than others," he said, wishing for nothing more than a quiet retreat to the gatehouse after this. His unfinished work—the plays and birthday ode—were ever before him.

"I've heard you're something of a recluse," she said as if sensing his present mood. "No wonder you traded the allure of London for the lush if sleepy Lowlands."

"A recluse? I don't deny it."

"Lady Marchmont invited Mother and I for tea day before yesterday. She spoke of neighboring Berwick families including you Humes and expressed her surprise you'd returned."

Lady Marchmont…Nicola Lockhart. The realization brought immediate indigestion. "I haven't seen the lady in question in years."

"She said that you were once quite close to her sister who is now an invalid after some unfortunate accident."

Maryn. An invalid. With an inward wince, Orin pinned his gaze on a deep ditch in the distance akin to the course this conversation was taking. Again he wondered the nature of her injuries. Was she no longer able to enjoy outings like this? Or did she choose to shut herself away from the world for other reasons?

Miss Lyon darted a searching glance at him. "I don't mean to pry, of course, but one can't help but wonder the association. *Quite close* implies something other than friendship."

Did it? Miss Lyon was nothing if not direct. While he preferred it to subterfuge, he thought it a less than charming trait in a lass he didn't ken well. He abhorred blather. And he wasn't about to contribute to it.

Tabula rasa. A clean slate.

That was what he wanted. And so he said nothing, just continued to eat his meal in thoughtful silence. But he sensed her discomfiture. Her desire to dig deeper. And it called out his own stubbornness to stay guarded.

Maryn vowed to forget Orin Hume and lose herself in her literary pursuits. She'd neglected them of late and so turned to the half-finished play she'd been working on atop Grandfather's desk. Only it wasn't quite where she'd left it. The new maid was to blame, she guessed. Both a footman and maidservant had been hired since she'd decided to stay on at Lockhart Hall. The latter, a lass from Duns, seemed more tapsalteerie than tidy, but if Mrs. Duncan wasn't complaining then Maryn wouldn't either. Capable servants were hard to come by.

Finally, she found the play beneath a book at the desk's edge. Inking a quill, she scribbled a few lines before giving up altogether. Today, at least, Lord Folderol and Lady Cowslip failed to hold her attention. A drastic happening in a play. If the author was indifferent the audience would be, too. Time to bring the curtain down for now.

That last letter in the secret drawer... it wouldn't let her be.

Perhaps if she read it and moved past it she could return to her usual endeavors. Life seemed largely upside down since she'd become duchess. A new title. A change in residence. Acrimony from her estranged sister. She'd sent the girls a tea set and other toys after their visit, hoping it would facilitate goodwill. But she'd received neither acknowledgment nor thanks. Nicola, she remembered, had never been good at either.

Her heart beat faster as she took out the final letter. A sennight had passed since Orin's unexpected visit. She'd not been back to the cottage but stayed on at the Hall, her nerves ragged at the possibility he might return. The purpose of his visit gnawed at her like the unread letter. Her fingers fairly shook retrieving it.

My dearest Maryn,

'Tis the close of another year and the month of Herschel's grievous loss. I have one more letter in me and then I will leave off unless I hear from you. The past months have given me time to decide on a course of action after being largely at sea since the tragedy. Not knowing where or how you are is another reason I need to move forward.

The laird, has recommended a change in location for me. I have decided to move to London in the new year and accept the invitation of Dr. Samuel Fancourt to assist with his new circulating library and bookshop there. Given that, I don't want to leave Scotland nor leave you in doubt about my abiding affection for you or my whereabouts though I do not blame you for withholding yours.

If you or your family have need of anything I will leave London at the first summons. You have my heart, both now and always, no matter what has transpired in the past or should happen in future.

Your entire,
Orin Hume

She looked up and through the window glass to the garden. Rose petals blew about in a merry dance in the rising wind but she hardly saw them.

You have my heart, both now and always.

Even now, Orin, after a silence that signified I cared nothing for you in return?

His poignant words reminded her of the Hume coat of arms which read in Latin...

True to the end.

16

Wedderburn Castle's two-story stable block held a great many cobwebs and hay-scented shadows. The late July sun poked through in places, helping Orin recover a key piece of his childhood from the carriage house. Amused, the stable hands watched him roll the well-worn contraption out of its stall then quickly returned to their work when the laird appeared.

"What the devil … " Everard began, dressed for riding. "I've not seen that conveyance in an age."

"The auld pony cart." Orin stood back and surveyed the wooden frame with its wrought-iron accents and cracked leather seat. The blue paint was admirably intact but he was less sure of the spoked wheels.

"You and Blythe used to cavort all over the parish in that cheeky chariot. And not only Blythe."

Nay, not only. He needed no reminder. Orin bent and inspected the axles while the laird circled and eyed the cart from all angles. Once upon a time he and Maryn had logged miles over all of Berwick. She preferred the cart to sidesaddle as she'd not been the horsewoman her brother, Herschel, was. A riding mishap had shaken her long before the sleigh accident.

Everard stooped and examined the wheels. "The rims look solid but I'd have the wheelwright check the remainder."

Orin tested the footrest. "I intend to take it out again."

Everard sent him a canny look. "With my countess ... or the Duchess of Fordyce?"

Orin smiled wryly. He'd never been able to dupe his eldest brother. "I might attempt the latter but am not sure I'll succeed."

"Try the former first and pray about the rest." With that, the laird strode away to where a groom waited with his own mount. The sound of retreating hoofbeats echoed as Everard rode west.

Climbing into the cart, Orin sat and stared at the empty whip socket. He and Maryn had always taken turns with the reins. His Highland pony, Brodie, had been a capable, patient beast. But did the Wedderburn stables have a replacement?

"Ye've a choice between a robust Fell pony from Northumberland or a Dales pony trained for cart driving," the stable master told him. "Either would suit. The laird makes sure we have plenty of horses on hand for all sorts of purposes."

But first, a thorough inspection of the cart itself. Over the next few days Orin took time making repairs along with the wheelwright, even installing a new leather seat. The paint he left alone. He didn't want the cart to look too different.

The countess was on hand to test it out. Once seated, Blythe sighed with delight. "This brings back a hundred happy memories."

"I recall I was too peely-wally back then to sit a horse so the cart sufficed."

She laughed. "Few would believe it now. Look at you, every bit as stalwart as the laird—and by far the tallest Hume!"

Chuckling, he ran a hand down the Fell pony's—Half-Penny's—broad back before taking the reins. They soon left the stable yard and ambled down the drive the laird had taken to the west gates. The clement day held low clouds and a cooling breeze that carried from the coast.

"Everard said you might take this to Lockhart Hall." Blythe pulled her hat lower to shield her eyes from the sun. "If so, a charming gesture."

"I haven't decided." In truth, he was no closer to deciding than when he'd first pulled the cart from its stall.

"You aren't afraid to take chances. One of your many admirable traits."

"Admirable? I'm not sure my heart is up to the risk. Or hers."

"Ah, hearts. Half-broken but soon mended, I hope."

He guided the pony into a turn that led onto the main road to Duns. "God forbid I do anything I regret."

"Or regret you did nothing," she replied sagely. "Which is worse?"

He'd considered that. Being haunted by inaction seemed crueler than outright rejection even twice. First Maryn's lack of response to his letters. And now her possible refusal of his unexpected arrival in a pony cart.

"So, I've been praying more lately . . . " The admission pained him after a long season of prayerlessness. "And the pony cart came to mind. I hadn't thought of it in years."

"Perhaps this is your answer, then. Often the Lord leads us step by step. A walk of faith, truly. Or in this case, a ride of faith."

"Much easier to just venture to the Hall atop Septimus."

"This cart has a history. You two began riding around in it when quite young. Maryn couldn't pronounce your name so she called you *Orry* so sweetly. Her mother was a dear friend of mine, remember. We were often together in those days. I was overcome when she and Maryn's father died. But I digress." She reached up to steady her hat in a sudden breeze. "If Maryn suffered injuries as has been rumored, she may not be able to ride a horse so this is likely preferable, and very thoughtful."

He fell silent. Maryn had called him Orry on many occasions even full grown. It was one of the things he most missed, those subtle intimacies they'd shared. As far as her injuries, they haunted him. So many questions rolled round his head day and night. Even after all this time they hadn't abated. He wasn't able, like many, to just close that chapter of his life and move on. An old soul, his nurse had said since childhood. He lived on another level. Sometimes he wanted to curse his romantic nature. His ability to experience life deeply. Maryn had been even more sensitive than he, so easily moved by the world around her.

Was she still?

"He's here, Your Grace!" The urgency in the new maid's voice brought Maryn downstairs in a dither.

"Who?" she asked, putting a hand to her disheveled hair. Rosemary was away on an errand and Maryn always felt quite unkempt without her.

"A gentleman." Alice peered out the door's sidelight. "Driving a bonny blue cart!"

"Turn him away, then, please." Collecting herself, Maryn passed into the library and then to the security of her cabinet, refusing a look out the window. Immediately she rued her reaction.

Could it be Orin?

Her hands began to tremble which mirrored her insides, aquiver like quince jelly. She could hear a slight commotion in the forecourt and then a footman opening the front door. Had the servants not heard they were to refuse him? Where had Alice gone?

"This way, Mr. Hume."

Losh! Maryn whirled in the doorway of the cabinet to face him. Her companion since childhood. The enduring love of her girlhood. Now an estranged man who caused her heart to beat so hard she felt it to her thudding temples.

"Your Grace." Orin gave a courtly bow surely perfected in London's choicest drawing rooms.

Maryn simply stared—and stopped her unsteady knees from bending to a ludicrous curtsey in the nick of time. *That* was the effect he had on her. Up close, he looked as magnificent as she felt disheveled. Clad in a blue and black tartan coat and dark breeches, every inch of him was finely tailored but not over-played. Time had done nothing to diminish his presence. He reminded her of the laird only Everard was almost twice his age. The man before her was in his prime and had his best years before him.

She swallowed past the lump knotting her throat. He waited for her to speak and she finally choked out two nearly inaudible words. "Mr. Hume."

His gaze moved to the bookshelves as if giving her time to collect herself.

An impossibility.

"I remember being in this room," he said easily. "There was an illustrated book about Berwick legends we used to pore over."

Taking a breath, she went to the very shelf. Grandfather hadn't altered the library, thankfully. She took it and held it out to him since she didn't trust herself to take so much as a step—or even speak.

He strode across the carpet in those striking black riding boots with cognac-colored cuffs and took the tiny tome from her. She held her breath and turned so that her injured limb was half-hidden in the folds of her petticoats.

"Though I confess I'm not here to read but to ride," he said, thumbing through the worn pages. "If you'll accept the humble invitation and our prior pony cart."

Our. He was as charming as he was braw. And she was melting faster than the ice house in midsummer. "Mr. Hume, I..."

He closed the book and met her hesitant gaze. His invitation stood. How could she refuse him? Those impossibly blue eyes. A Hume blue, some said. Blue as forget-me-nots...

She took the book back and hugged it to her bodice. "Why have you come?"

His eyes held raw regret. "Because it's been too long."

That did indeed sum it up. "We were close companions once but times—things—have altered."

"Only if we let them."

She returned the book to the shelf. "I would need to change and my maid is not here." A lame excuse. He said nothing and so she looked to the carpet where sunlight illuminated the pretty pattern and a worn thread or two.

"Once the pony cart amused you. I find it worthwhile still." Far from being put off by her dithering and dallying, he continued patient. Kind. As thoughtful as she remembered. His hopeful silence undermined her resolve.

"A short ride then." A measly mile or two. Yet she was already ruing her answer.

"As you wish."

She excused herself and fled upstairs. Alice was nowhere to be seen so she put on a bergère hat and gloves. Had he noticed her injury? He was waiting outside when she reappeared and passed through the open front door. The sight of the pony cart, once so beloved, lanced her. She could hardly see it through her tears and realized she had no handkerchief.

He handed her up and she lowered herself to the new leather seat though all the rest of the conveyance seemed remarkably unchanged. With expert movements he guided the pony—a bonny, young creature—beyond the forecourt. A breeze cooled her flushed face as she looked to the gates in the distance, the wrought iron as stiff as she felt.

Amid the warm sun and the rustling lime trees and the cart's gentle swaying, she fought to keep her emotions in check. As he slowed their pace to minimize the dust she nearly changed her mind and got out of the cart. If only she could return to the lass she'd been, when sitting beside him was entirely natural. Now he seemed entirely too close. So close she caught his citrus-sage scent, reminding her of his card tucked away in her cabinet. She refused to look at him and further ensnare her heart so she fastened her gaze on the landscape.

They were nearing Lockhart Hall's ornate entrance. When Orin turned right onto the main road toward the coast she held her peace. Let them have it out, whatever this was. Then they could move on with their lives.

"Why are you here and not in London?"

"How did you know where I was?" Amusement laced his words.

She almost smiled. "Britain's Poet Laureate is hard to hide."

"Which is one reason I returned home."

"Scotland is still home, then."

"Now and hopefully in future, aye. I've taken up residence in the gatehouse."

"The gatehouse?" She nearly sighed as a dozen poignant recollections took hold. In her girlish dreams she'd often wished they could live there. Together. "'Tis a charming place. I remember the walled garden fondly. What made you leave the Court?"

"Sheer boredom to begin with."

"The Scottish Lowlands is the epitome of that for many."

"But not for you nor me."

"Never." She kept her gaze between the pony's upright ears and the little traveled, brown ribbon of road.

All the while she marveled. Riding about unchaperoned while in mourning violated every convention she knew. Yet he was bold enough to buck custom and she had thrown caution to the wind and let him. If they went much further they'd not return till sunset.

As if reading her thoughts, he halted on a particularly picturesque knoll. Fast Castle was visible despite its crumbling splendor, heather purpling the moors in all directions, the blue backdrop of sea breathtaking. For a moment she forgot her turmoil.

"Why did you seek me out today?" She spoke so quietly it seemed the wind might fling her words away. "I'm sure it wasn't just to ride me around in a pony cart."

When he took his time answering she stole a look at him, as if she could reconcile the young man he'd been to the older man he was becoming. Were those glints of silver in his dark blonde hair? If so, it turned him all the more braw.

She nearly shuddered at the next thought. What did he see when he looked at her after being amongst the most beautiful, titled women in Britain? She shrank from the comparison. Duchess or no, she could never be the lady on his arm at Court. She couldn't even befriend him in Berwickshire. Not at the risk to her heart. Or his reputation.

"I came to see how you are. If you have need of anything," he finally said, eyes on the view. "I wasn't sure you'd even see me."

I wouldn't have if the new maid had followed my directions.

"I rarely see anyone," she confessed by way of apology.

Yet part of her wanted desperately to change that, to make up for lost time and tell him everything. Explain away five years and reveal she'd found his letters and thereby realized he'd not received hers. So much lay hidden in her heart and head that begged sharing.

But to what purpose?

She looked down at her gloved arm hanging limply by her side. "Grandfather's death flushed me out of hiding, so to speak."

"Why hide?" he asked gently.

"My injury and five years of mourning allow for little else. It does seem something of a curse to lose a brother, then parents, and lately a grandfather in that span of time."

"Not the Lockhart curse, Maryn ... a fallen world."

Maryn. She was growing so used to her new title that she'd forgotten how intimate forenames were. She'd yet to say *Orin*—wouldn't let herself say it. And she mustn't say *Orry* ever.

He continued on, quietly, "Since we're close neighbors, I'd have us be on good terms, at least."

"Distant neighbors, rather." Though it hurt, she forced a coldness into her tone she was far from feeling. "I want nothing, thank you. Nor do I need your pity if that forms the basis of your visit."

17

It had ever been Maryn's way, when out of her depth, to resort to a chilling insincerity. Such seemed particularly false in light of her usual graciousness. Yet her stilted words still struck deep. The battle between them had begun when he'd stood before her in Lockhart Hall's library. Her battle, anyway. Orin nearly admitted defeat the moment he'd looked at her stricken face.

The injury she'd tried to hide he'd noticed immediately, along with the slight slump to her normally straight shoulders as if intent on shrinking from sight. Aside from being more rounded than he remembered, she was even more beautiful. Her hair was still her glory, a shining wealth of blue-black even wind-whipped. Stray wisps dangled here and there, making him want to reach out and tuck them away. But it was her green eyes he'd remember if he never saw her again. Not lively and shining but listless... haunted.

"Pity," he finally said, "is the least of my motivations."

"Whatever your reasons, I beg you return me home."

"I'd rather show you the gatehouse and garden. Once it was your favorite place."

She hesitated. "Even if I wanted to, there's no going back to what was."

He looked at her. He was having a hard time looking away from her. "We'll make a new start then."

"Much has happened since Herschel's death." Her eyes glittered. "Much I cannot speak of."

The catch in her voice made his own throat tighten. He fisted the slack reins when what he wanted was to take her in his arms and shoulder the brunt of her pain. His mind began sifting through her wounded words to what might lie beneath. It was challenging scaling the formidable wall she'd been erecting from the first though he felt no frustration. He felt time was running out. If he didn't deal with her honestly, attempt to mend their estrangement, he feared he'd not have another chance.

His angst doubled when she said, "I'd rather you return to the lady I saw you with from my coach."

So, she'd been thinking of a lass he hardly thought about? Myriad possibilities ricocheted through his mind. Might her mentioning Miss Lyon indicate a deeper feeling for him than she was willing to acknowledge?

"You shouldn't have sought me out." Her troubled eyes met his again. "I don't want you to do so again."

Hard as it was to hear, he understood. "If this has to do with the past—if my presence pains you—then I will leave you be."

Without answering, she got out of the cart and walked toward the cliff's edge. Her hat nearly took wing in a sudden burst of wind and she was trying to hold down her skirts with her good hand. Should he go after her? For a moment he feared she'd fall—or worse.

Lord Almighty, help.

He climbed out, ready to catch her—or comfort her. "Maryn."

His gut lurched when she turned toward him, tears tracing her pale face. He wanted to take her in his arms. Dry her tears. Be what she needed, whatever that was. Reluctantly, she took the handkerchief he offered. He didn't dare touch her—

"I'm sorry." She made a wide circle around him to return to the cart, her voice so full of feeling it shook. "I'm not the Maryn you remember, not one whit. And I can't pretend otherwise. Please return me home now."

Orin rode to Duns the next day, the village he'd known all his life. He needed to do something to clear his head if not his heart after his failure at Lockhart Hall. Below the hulk of Duns Castle on the hill, the main square was chock-full of horses and wagons, the weekly market anchoring Lowland life. After a tankard of ale at the *Ewe and Lamb,* he made his way to Black Bull Street and the empty building he'd had his eye on since his arrival back in Berwickshire.

The empty shop's stone face boasted two bow-fronted windows, the grimy glass in need of cleaning. To his right was an apothecary, to his left a tailor. Both respectable and well-established. A gentleman who was none other than Lord Lyon left the latter and greeted him heartily.

"Milord," the older man began with a wink, no doubt referencing the rejected baronetcy. "What brings you to town?"

"A business matter. I've had my eye on this building since my return."

"Whatever for?"

"To found a circulating library."

Lord Lyon looked amused. Nay, scornful. "Hardly worthy of an earl's son, is it?"

Orin held his peace, well aware his cause was often unpopular among the gentry.

"The lower classes aren't meant to read, surely," he persisted. "They're meant to labor and laborers don't require any sort of education. My opinion is that by educating the masses you'll only encourage them to aspire to the unattainable."

"I didna ask your opinion," Orin said evenly, looking over the shop's front to see if a sign to sell or let was posted. "Nor do I agree with it."

"Be that as it may, Hume, your mission is more fool's errand."

"Fool's errand or nae, Lowland literacy has long been my aim. For now, I'm here to determine this empty building's owner."

"Oh? 'Tis Fordyce property, from what I've heard. The duchy owns most of this street, in fact. But since the auld duke died things may have changed hands."

Fordyce property? If he'd leveled him with a blow Orin couldn't have been more taken aback. Or determined.

"I'll look into it, then," he said, thanking him.

Lord Lyon turned away. "I ne'r figured you for a merchant, Hume."

The slur was not lost on him. "An enlightened commercial venture, mayhap."

"How did it go at Lockhart Hall?"

If anyone other than Blythe had asked him, Orin would have considered it a sore subject. The countess, however, always tread lightly and her genuine concern assuaged him.

"Not well," He sat down beside her in the shade of a wisteria arbor like they'd done since he was a lad. She still spent much of her time outdoors in fair weather.

"I don't mean to pry but I am praying."

"Bethankit. I've spent many years seeing answers to your prayers."

"How is she?"

"Wounded." He mulled their regrettable meeting. "Her left side seems to have taken the brunt of the accident. Other than that she's as bonny as ever, at least outwardly. Her spirits are another matter."

"Too much loss, I fear. And now the entire weight of the duchy on her shoulders."

"She made it clear she doesn't want to see me again though she did ride with me to that overlook where you can see clear to Fast Castle and the North Sea."

"Surely riding with you in that restored cart counts for something," she told him consolingly. "I admire your efforts. Not many would attempt such."

The dreamer in him had hoped for a different sort of reunion. A glimmer of the lass he once knew. His mind remained fixed on their chilling silence when he'd returned her home. Had sadness and suffering changed her irrevocably?

"Perhaps I should invite her here for tea now that we know where she is."

"I'm going to try a different tack." Orin leaned back and folded his arms across his chest, a tentative plan taking shape. "Approach her about a business venture."

"Truly? What on earth do you have up your sleeve?"

"A circulating library which may well include a print shop. Ironically enough, the building is owned by the new duchess."

"How fortuitous." Blythe's surprise turned to delight. "She's as literary minded as you and always has been. Perhaps this venture—a joint venture—will be what you both need."

"You're far more confident than I. She may not be willing to let the building to me, let alone sell. She may even feel the cart ride I took her on was a cunning means to an end."

"Not if she knows you well though I do wish you'd been able to deal with the business matter first." Blythe worried the pearl ring on her finger, her usual serenity ruffled. "But there's no undoing what's been done. When will you approach her?"

"I'm undecided. Pray about that too, aye?"

Lord Lovell took Orin aside into an alcove at the next fête. "A word with you if I may. I leave for Edinburgh on my father's business tomorrow but want to ask for Lady Charis's hand first."

"Have you approached the laird?"

Lovell expelled a tense breath. "I had planned on it tonight but he was summoned to Jedburgh on some matter."

"Does Charis ken your intentions?"

"She does but says her father wants her to finish the season first."

"You should respect that then." Orin wished otherwise but it seemed the course of true love never did run smoothly. "Everard is not a man to cross as a future son-in-law."

"Agreed. I'm not worried about the laird but all the other suitors vying for her hand while I'm away, namely Lords Lindsay and Keith."

"If you're certain of her affections then you need not be concerned with any rivals." Orin looked toward the ballroom floor where Charis was indeed dancing with Lindsay. "From where I'm standing you have none."

"My frequent absences and my father's failing health put me in a precarious position, at least where courting is concerned." He grimaced, darting another look in Charis's direction. "Society with all its innuendo and protocol wears one down. I'd as soon revert to medieval times when knights wore the colors of the lady they were fighting for around their arms."

"You echo Iago in *Othello*." It had been one of many plays he and Maryn had learned line by line long ago. *"But I will wear my heart upon my sleeve."*

"Aye, I am hopelessly romantically entangled, heart upon my sleeve for all to see," Lovell murmured, warning in his gaze. "And not only I, my friend..."

He slipped away, leaving Orin with a frowning, fan-fluttering Miss Lyon. "You've only partnered with me once all evening, Mr. Hume, and 'tis nearly midnight."

"This evening is more about business than pleasure, I'm afraid."

"Ah, yes." Her fan fluttered harder. "Father said you're gauging interest in this new Lowland endeavor of yours and that you've run against some opposition."

"Only from those who won't acknowledge the merits of being literate." Lord Lyon foremost, he didn't add. "There are some here who even say the plays and novels of this age will corrupt those who read them."

"Rather ironic given you're a playwright and poet." She sighed. "I confess our library at Lyon Court is rather lacking. We'd rather pursue other interests. If I agreed to frequent your future bookshop, might you make time for a foxhunt or two?"

Orin's half-smile softened his stance. "I'll be too busy for sporting in future if all goes as planned. And I'll have little time for dancing."

"Well, we'll have to make tonight memorable then. As for my father, not everyone agrees with his opinions. I applaud you for pursuing something different given your bookish bent. And I'll cheer you on in any way that I can."

18

*O*f all she'd given up being one-handed, embroidery and watercolors remained. With the weather so fair, Maryn had a chaise readied to return to the knoll Orin had shown her a fortnight ago. There she took her album of papers, a paintbox, and brushes while the new footman fetched water for her from a nearby burn. He then, as she encouraged, went fishing, leaving her to her own devices.

At first she sat, hands in her lap, and took in the view she'd not been able to focus on with any purpose or intent when Orin had sat so close beside her. Alone, the landscape unfolded before her in all its summer splendor, a slight wind toying with her hat ribbons. If she expected to feel more serene today, she didn't. Since she'd sent him away rather ungraciously, she'd not had a moment's peace.

Forgive me, Lord.

The confession seemed to clear her head and restore her creativity somewhat. Picking up a lead pencil, she began to sketch with her good hand, only she didn't draw the stunning landscape before her but something else entirely. Once she had the proportions in place she took up a fine brush to flesh out the features, blending and building till she was somewhat satisfied.

A well-sculpted jaw. Straight nose and chiseled cheekbones. Intelligent, expressive eyes. Carefully queued hair of a hue that escaped her completely. And a self-assured demeanor imbued with a humility that could never be replicated.

Her feeble paints and brushes didn't do Orin Hume justice by half.

Not even Hogarth himself could capture the essence of the man she'd known her entire life. In the sun and wind, the paper dried quickly. Once it did, she covered it with a cloth to keep it from the eyes of the footman who was still fishing. Now she could savor the view and only hope her humble portrait would help expunge the longing she felt for the man she could never call hers.

Maryn returned to Lockhart Hall and unwelcome news.

"Yer Grace," Alice greeted her, unnervingly impish. "Mr. Hume called again in the forenoon. He seemed sair-hearted to nae find ye home ... so I told him ye'd return by tea time."

"You didn't!" Maryn clutched the covered watercolor to her bodice, feeling a flaming hypocrite.

"He has a way about him, ye ken," Alice murmured with an apologetic curtsey.

Oh aye, I ken that well enough, Maryn didn't say, coming to a standstill in the tiled foyer.

"My apologies, Your Grace." Mrs. Duncan appeared, more shamefaced than Maryn had ever seen her. "I was preoccupied belowstairs with another matter entirely and left Alice unsupervised briefly. I never expected visitors."

"Please, think no more of it, either of you." Bemused, Maryn hurried to her cabinet to hide her artwork.

In her discomfiture she'd forgotten to tell the servants *not* to prepare tea. Four o'clock followed—and Mr. Hume. Even Rosemary was all a-titter.

"Here he comes…" She abandoned pinning up Maryn's hair to peer out the second-floor bedchamber window with a rare squeal of delight. "Riding a bold black stallion. Like a knight in a fairytale!"

Shaken, Maryn felt far removed from a fairytale as she came down the staircase and found he'd been shown into the small drawing room. At once she realized the error. Alice's doing? The cherry-red chamber was cozy, even intimate, and was *not* what was called for.

Orin turned toward her as she entered, her sable skirts rustling. She felt abominable in black. It mirrored her present mood. His refined bow again reminded her of another impossible chasm between them.

"Mr. Hume." She kept her voice cool if cordial.

"I hope I'm not interrupting, Your Grace." Hat in hand, he seemed the picture of romantic entreaty.

"You're just in time for refreshments," she said graciously, determined to make the best of it.

Alice entered as if on cue, delivering a silver tray so sumptuously laden it surely rivaled Kensington Palace. They'd not finish such a spread in a sennight. Maryn felt a flush from her slippered feet to her lace cap as they both sat, the tea table between them.

"You've not brought your pony cart," she said lightly as she poured him coffee from an octagonal silver pot.

"More business than pleasure today," he replied, adding sugar and a splash of cream to his cup. Just as she remembered.

"Business? I'm intrigued."

His brilliant blue eyes met hers and she quite forgot everything they'd just said. *Heaven help me.* Her good hand shook as she poured tea for herself.

"I don't want you to think my prior visit was anything but pleasure," he told her with that beguiling intensity he had. "Though it may not have been that for you."

"Our recent reunion was unexpected." She bit her lip, adding sugar and cream to her own cup. "And I'm not good with the unexpected."

"Once you were."

"As I said last time, I'm not the lass you remember."

"I beg to differ. She's simply hidden beneath hardship and hurt."

Point taken. He'd summed her up in a trice but…Eyes down, she took a sip of tea as he continued.

"So, I have in mind a bookshop and circulating library here in the Lowlands. In Duns, actually."

"Like Ramsay's in Edinburgh?" She continued to regard her teacup instead of him. "We visited once, remember?"

And what a visit it had been. An autumn day overflowing with bookshops and hot cross buns and foaming flip in a cross west wind. She and Herschel had stayed at the Hume's Canongate mansion with Orin and Charis. Nicola had been missing. Her sister didn't care for the city nor books.

"One of my best memories." He reached for a bannock. "Like Ramsay's, aye. Mayhap a printing press in time. But there needs to be a building first."

"Of course." She tried to imagine it. He'd certainly outdistanced her in regards to vision. She'd never thought of a bookshop in Duns.

"Lowland towns are growing rapidly. Access to books—a library—will help with literacy and reach those who've not been able to benefit from the written word. Many here cannot afford so much as a simple primer."

"I support you wholeheartedly," she said, finding better footing with a business venture. "But how am I to be of help?"

"You own a building in Duns that would suffice."

She sat back. "I do?"

His amusement led to her own. "Aye, a whole lane of them."

A flush warmed her all over again. "I'm only just learning the extent of Grandfather's holdings and feel quite ignorant."

"You have an able factor or steward, I hope."

"Grandfather's first footman is attempting to turn steward which should make a satisfactory arrangement. I ken little of estate matters though I do enjoy visiting tenants." Already she was anticipating her next visit. She especially loved the bairns. "As for your future shop, I will gladly let the building or you could purchase, whichever suits your purposes."

If he bought it, their business association would be at an end. To let it would mean it would continue. Her heart bade her let it but—

"I'd rather purchase," he said matter-of-factly.

She poured him more coffee and the repast dwindled as they grew quiet. She could, however, sense the machinations of both their minds. Never in a hundred years did she dream they'd sit here discussing such a matter. All the possibilities and repercussions of a Berwickshire bookshop and future print shop seemed endless. A wee light flickered inside her. Hope?

"Then I shall look into it," she told him, sampling a raisin-studded scone though she'd lost her appetite.

"You are quite occupied, I imagine, with the duchy and all it entails."

"I lack a business mind. I would rather spend my time in your future bookshop."

"If the plan moves forward you are welcome there any time you please."

"You would hire shopkeepers? I'm guessing the building would have to be thoroughly transformed and refinished with shelves. Books. And there would need to be a catalogue of all the books, besides."

"And you say you've no head for business." His wry expression suggested otherwise.

She bit her lip to keep from saying she'd enjoy cataloguing the books. What books? He didn't say he had any yet and she wouldn't rush the process. She must keep her involvement to a minimum. Let him move forward on his own. Orin Hume's place in her life was in the past. Period.

Orin drank a second cup of coffee, debating if now was the time to broach the subject closest to his heart or just leave this meeting a business matter. Maryn seemed less resistant this time, less so than on their cart ride. But he could still see she was easily over-whelmed. Skittish. Reluctant to meet his eyes. Not the smiling, carefree lass of before.

Leave off, man.

It was unfair of him to keep comparing her to who she'd been. Mayhap he was wrong to say the old Maryn was simply buried beneath. He wasn't even the man he'd been five years ago. Time alone changed one and all.

"I've taken enough of your time," he finally said, finished with what had been the most abundant repast he'd had in recent memory.

She'd had several cups of tea herself so clearly he'd outstayed his welcome. Yet he read something akin to disappointment in her eyes. Or was he imagining it?

"I shall contact Grandfather's solicitors about a possible purchase," she said thoughtfully. "And once I discover what is required I'll have them contact you directly."

He nodded, suddenly at a loss about how to end this second meeting. He was even more at a loss to explain his emotions. What he felt defied description. He was too aware of her, caught in a swelling tangle of regret, longing, and who knew what else.

Naething can our wilder passions tame.

His fellow poet, Allan Ramsay, had said it well.

Still, time apart might bring clearer perspective.

In a fortnight the contract had been drawn up and the Black Bull Street purchase would soon be his. Orin even had keys handed him by an Edinburgh solicitor, leaving Maryn out of the transaction completely. His heart said it was regrettable while his head insisted it was wise. Standing in the empty building with the laird, he considered what needed doing next.

"Since I'm helping finance this affair I have a say, aye?" Everard walked the first floor then bumped his head as he ascended to the second story. "You'll need wooden shelves of all dimensions. A desk and chairs. Printing presses if you desire to continue this madness and manufacture your own materials. An apprentice or two and account books in spades."

"All of it, aye." Orin ducked as his own head barely missed a low beam. "I can already smell the ink, leather, and paper."

"Such a dreamer ye are," Everard all but scoffed though his wink softened his severity. "The new duchess gave you nae trouble?"

"None." Orin ran a hand along a scarred wall in need of paint. "Why would she?"

"Because this isn't simply commerce." The laird took a Windsor chair by a window as if intent on discussing the matter. "I ken you're still besotted with her though she's now beyond you're reach."

Besotted. Guilty. Beyond his reach? That barefaced fact stung. Only Blythe seemed to disagree. Another unwanted realization dawned. "Meaning every titled bachelor in existence will be at her doorstep when her mourning ends."

The laird heaved a rare sigh. "She's a beauty—or was—and now she's worth a fortune. A double blessing or a blight, however you look at it."

Was a beauty? Time had only turned Maryn more bonny, at least in his eyes. The bloom of her youth had matured into something far richer and more refined. But he couldn't dwell on that long. Best keep himself in hand and not give way to these fiery bursts of feeling. Everard had rightly branded him besotted.

A sudden banging shut of the lower shop door brought Charis upstairs. "Father, there you are! I fretted you'd be impatiently waiting outside the dressmaker's window." She brushed dust off her lace sleeve. "What is this I hear of Lady Maryn?"

"We were discussing her many attributes," the laird said.

"Rather the suitors who will besiege her once she sheds her sable."

Dusting off a windowseat with a handkerchief, Charis sat. "There are some frightful fortune hunters who, I hear, already have her in their sights."

Orin's hackles rose. Rakes and fortune hunters aside, he was far from comfortable with even a worthy suitor winning Maryn's hand. "You've heard what exactly?"

"Moving in society like I do, everyone and everything is discussed, especially when it comes to the Lockharts and their supposedly accursed past." Her lovely face drew up in distaste. "Lord Blackadder, for one, has his eye on her, or rather her fortune. Also, Sir Lionel—and the Frenchman, Larmamond. Vultures, all. She's especially vulnerable given she has no family near except an estranged sister."

Orin crossed his arms. "She needs allies. Trusted companions." Something rotten as well as protective of her ate at his core. The *green-eyed monster* as Shakespeare said. Jealousy?

"We invited the duchess for tea at Wedderburn last week. Sadly, she politely declined and sent a lovely bouquet of those heirloom Lockhart Hall roses Mama's always admired instead."

"But tea in a private home is well within the constraints of mourning," Orin said. "Especially in the countryside."

"Of course." She looked at him sympathetically, seeming older than her years. "I think it had to do with something else entirely."

Tamping down his roiling emotions, Orin tried to focus on practicalities within his control such as all the candles needed to run such an establishment as this. A fortune's worth of wax. Could it be done?

"What are you going to call this place, Uncle?" Charis's mercurial mood shifted yet again. "*Hume's Circulating Library? The Wedderburn Bookshop?*"

"I've nae idea." A careless shrug to his shoulders belied the heaviness in his chest. "Something literary yet respectable, mayhap."

"*The Duchess's Literary Delight?*" She winked, so like her father Orin almost smiled. "I can picture the sign hanging outside embellished with a tiara and book."

Orin shot down the whimsical notion. "Rather *The Poor Poet's Tome of Literary Treasure.*"

She laughed and motioned them both downstairs with a gloved hand. "'Tis getting late. We must be away lest Mama wonder what befell us."

19

August arrived, the landscape assuming the burnt look of late summer. Temperatures rose and Maryn spent the warmest days inside, trying to learn more about the duchy and, in idle moments, embroider. A letter came from her London publisher, telling her the Poet Laureate's newest play had been chosen over hers for the new theatrical season. She rejoiced privately. How could she begrudge the man she most admired?

One look at the calendar told her it had been over a fortnight since Orin's visit and business proposition. Her solicitor told her the matter would soon be finalized and had also sent her a letter informing her of the sale of Grandfather's London townhouse. She perused it now, every unbelievable line. The buyer didn't want the furniture nor the library. What did she want to do?

Not want the library?

She knew who would. Stunned, she sat back. But it would require her involvement once again. And inevitably her heart.

Maryn took a chaise to Wedderburn's gatehouse, driven from curiosity as well as a desire to deliver the good news in person. A written note would have sufficed and been far safer. But her heart won out. Just one more meeting, she mused, as the conveyance rolled onto Wedderburn land just beyond the old stone gatehouse.

Was Orin even at home?

For a moment she just stood in the shade of an old oak, savoring her surroundings, the place of countless past escapades. A dozen different things vied for her attention, the gatehouse's garden foremost. It's ivy-clad walls beckoned and she caught the scent of flowers where she stood.

No longer did the place look forlorn or uninhabitable. Orin Hume had already left his mark. Muddied boots rested near a side door. A cocked hat hung from a peg. A gardener was at work, so old and bent he didn't seem to notice her arrival as he weeded the knot garden. Along the gatehouse wall came a striped cat, its tail wafting regally.

She felt extraordinarily... at home.

"Your Grace." The voice behind her made her turn.

"Please, no titles," she said as she faced the man who seemed to occupy her every waking thought and some nights her dreams. "Just plain Maryn."

"As you wish," Orin said, gesturing to the garden's open gate. "That will be all for today, Hayes."

The old gardener straightened as Orin thanked him then gave Maryn a brief bow before he disappeared. She went ahead of Orin into the garden, trying to tamp down her delight. It was even lovelier than before. Interwoven pathways led to a back bench that faced a cascading fountain. A marble statue of a child holding an open bird cage still stood amid clusters of blooming, swaying lavender. Today, in the sunlight, the winged creature on the child's shoulder assumed a poignancy it hadn't before and reminded Maryn of Orin's poem.

She waited till they were both seated before she handed him the Edinburgh solicitor's post. "As fate or Providence would have it, here is your library should you so desire."

He finished reading, befuddlement on his features. "At what cost?"

"A gift." She smiled, joy bubbling up in such a soul-expanding way she nearly lost her breath. "If that shop of yours can hold five thousand volumes."

"If?" His own smile bordered on the incredulous. He looked at her, holding her gaze so long it seemed to signify something other than mere celebration. "You may have to sell me a second building."

"Apparently the new owner has an extensive library and no need for Grandfather's," she explained. "Since Lockhart Hall's shelves are full I'd rather see the excess go to a worthy cause such as yours."

"I dinna ken what to say." He looked at the ground, clearly moved. "A fortune in books."

"I'll have them sent directly to your door in Duns if you like."

"Nae better plan." His eyes met hers again. "Promise me you'll visit. I'd like for you to see the shop before it opens."

She bit her lip, lost in the thought they were both happier than they'd been in a long time. Since Herschel's death, perhaps. At least she was. She couldn't speak for Orin though he looked happy, his wide smile calling out all the wee lines about his eyes.

"Of course I shall visit," she finally said.

20

Five thousand or so books? Orin could hardly take it in. The number exceeded Wedderburn's renowned library, quite a feat.

"You're sure?" he asked, searching her face for the slightest hint of indecision.

He found only a quiet joy. Suddenly even books were passe. Here he sat weighing whether to broach the subject of their prior romantic arrangement. Rather, a marriage contract. Yet Everard had reminded him a duchess was now out of his reach entirely. But not her books. He felt gutted and elated all at once.

"I'm happy to have found a home for them," she said, looking down at her gloved hands. "No one else would appreciate them like you."

He reached out and plucked a Damask rose. Making sure it was free of thorns, he extended it. "I owe you a great debt of gratitude."

She took the blossom and breathed in the heady fragrance. "If anyone owes anyone anything I owe you an explanation about your letters."

He paused, surprised. "That's all in the past, is it not?"

What's past is prologue, Shakespeare said. Truly, everything at present seems to hinge upon it. He waited on tenterhooks for her answer. She seemed overwhelmed again, weighing her words.

"Perhaps we'll both feel better if I tell you the truth of what happened." Vulnerability softened her lovely features. "You see, Grandfather didn't tell me you'd written after Herschel's death. In fact, he hid all your letters in a locked compartment of his desk, likely thinking I'd never find them. But I did find them recently, after his passing, which makes me wonder why. Now I'm questioning everything, including his doing so."

He listened to her torrent of words, sensing a torrent of tears behind them. Suddenly their situation had become even more complicated. "So, you thought I'd not written at all, never inquired about you or wondered where you'd gone."

She nodded and looked to her lap. "It seemed so unlike you, so contrary to our friendship."

Friendship, nay.

"What I felt for you was far from friendship," he said without thought, though speaking in the past tense helped remove them from the fraught present. "But I'm sure you gathered that from the letters. Six of them, if I remember rightly."

"Six, yes. I've read them all. More than once."

"Yet your silence at the time seemed to signify an ending of sorts."

He well remembered waiting and how agonizingly grey the days were without word from her. He wasn't a man given to excessive emotion, at least outwardly, but he'd felt a slow death when his hopes weren't realized and he never heard.

"But I did write." Her earnestness removed all doubt. "At first, I was too injured to pen but a few lines but in time I sent quite a few letters. Are we now to believe Grandfather withheld mine to you, too? If so, I do wonder what he did with them."

He focused on the slot in the garden wall that gaped empty, mirroring the still-empty part of himself that never seemed to recover. Physical wounds were bad enough. Mayhap those of the heart were worse.

"Does it make you angry?" he asked.

"More hurt." She bit her lip. "Bewildered. I still can't believe that Grandfather, a man of equal parts nobility and common sense, would have done such a thing."

"I had great respect for your grandfather but we'll never ken his actions. We can't undo what's been done. We just... let go. Go on."

"And so we have. Looking back, it seems we were little more than children then. Untried. Unchallenged. Unaccustomed to heartache. We've become different people. Taken different paths. Five years seems an age."

He regretted the grudging acceptance in her tone, as if she was trying to explain away what they'd had, like so much dust under the rug. "What did you make of my letters?"

Her smile was wistful. "Pure poetry, some of them. And the one about the birds... " Her voice faltered and she fastened on the fountain as it splashed water onto the mossy stones at its base. "I've committed every line to heart. It reminded me of this place with its uncaged songbird."

"I had that in mind when I wrote it." He, too, had memorized every line.

"Enough sentimentality." She got up so quickly the rose she'd been holding fell to her feet. She didn't retrieve it. "As you said, we let go. Go on."

He stood but she was at the garden gate before he caught up with her. Suddenly he felt as much at sea as a man half his age. And utterly gutted at her going. Much like he'd been when he'd never received her letters. To ground himself, he focused on her one-horse chaise, a fine equipage she somehow managed despite her injury.

Bidding her farewell, he helped her up then stood back and tried to reconcile himself to all they'd said.

And what they hadn't.

Maryn rode away with a sinking inside her mingled with confusion and an odd hope. What if she found those letters? If Grandfather had hidden Orin's, where might he have hidden hers? As the chaise turned onto the main road, leaving Wedderburn's gatehouse behind, she tried to recall those first weeks following the accident.

Grandfather, bless him, had secured the best medical care to be had in Edinburgh and London. Several doctors attended her, some from the medical school. The smell of camphor and her horror of bloodletting would never leave her. Nicola had been by her side night and day at first. She had a hazy memory of asking her sister to bring her ink and pounce and paper. In the beginning, it had taken all her strength to write a few sentences so her letters to Orin were stitched together over several days. Shattered, heartfelt letters that made her wince recalling them. They'd been written in the delirium of recovery before she'd known the full extent of her injuries.

Where had those impassioned pennings gone?

And why had she poured out herself to him? Aside from his letters, he'd never once, till today, told her his feelings were far from friendship. Nor had he ever kissed her. Back then she'd been unsure of his affection till the marriage settlement was broached between Grandfather and the laird. Only then had she an inkling Orin regarded her as something more.

Lately he seemed to seek her out because of courtesy and then business. Not only that, she still had the woman who'd gone riding with him firmly in mind. Though he never spoke of her, she continued to wonder.

Who was she?

21

When an invitation for tea arrived from Redbraes Castle, Maryn's surprise gave way to dread. She found her sister's company taxing and immediately suspected her motives. Usually one didn't hear from Nicola unless she wanted something. Would this be any different?

She considered sending her regrets as she'd done the very gracious invitation from Wedderburn Castle but the slight hope remained that she and Nicola might someday forge some sort of amicable bond. And if not with her sister, perhaps her nieces.

Taking the Lockhart coach due to the distance and the dust, Maryn tried to tamp down her nerves and enjoy the view through the open window. But that required passing by the Hume's gatehouse with all the accompanying angst.

Dear Orin, shall I ever get over you?

Her gaze fixed on the gable roof softened with moss and then the rear garden. She hadn't asked him if he recalled her leaving her other letters there. What had he done with all of them prior to the accident?

Any musings were short-lived as she soon arrived at Redbraes Castle, a place she'd never been. Gifted by Marchmont's late father upon their marriage, it boasted parklike grounds and a new Palladian wing. Imposing stone lions marked the forecourt.

Maryn alighted from the coach with a dry mouth and heavy heart, to say nothing of her queasiness.

A footman showed her to a drawing room crowded with ornate French-style furnishings. At once Maryn felt nearly suffocated by such busyness. Alas, she and Nicola were as different as night and day. And it suddenly dawned on her that her sister, with all her airs and graces, would have made a better duchess.

"How good of you to come." Nicola swept in, clad in lemon silk that cleverly disguised the coming Marchmont. "Please, have a seat."

However cordial her tone, Maryn detected a coldness therein. Were the girls near at hand? Her heart's wish was to see her three wee nieces but she didn't hear a sound.

Unsure of what to say, Maryn attempted to smile and sat at a table prepared for tea. Bread and butter topped a porcelain plate and the aroma of Bohea scented the air. A far cry from the feast Orin had been served during his visit to Lockhart Hall.

"If only the price of tea would fall," Nicola said, picking up a tarnished silver pot. "I am tiring of instructing the servants to re-use the leaves for their own pots though they make a fine cleaning aid sprinkled on carpets."

Maryn's brows arched. Were the Marchmonts so frugal? Again she wondered the state of their finances. "I hope the girls are enjoying the tiny tea set I sent."

"Enjoying? 'Genie broke a cup as soon as Lottie and Pen unpacked it." She poured the Bohea with a frown. "They seem to spend a lot of time fighting over who's to pour. Daughters can be so tiresome which is why I'm hoping for a son."

Maryn stirred sugar in her cup but spied no milk. "Not much longer now, your confinement?"

"A month more. Indigestion plagues me night and day. I rarely drink anything but mint tea though black tea is what I crave."

"Is anything needed for your lying in?" Maryn sipped the weak Bohea, craving coffee herself. "I'm happy to help in any way."

Nicola pursed her lips. "The christening will require some assistance. I may ask you to be the child's godmother."

Again, Maryn hid her surprise. Considering she hadn't known her nieces existed till recently, she'd not considered this. She suspected the honor had more to do with her being duchess and her sister's obsession with titles than any family feeling.

"Enough about me," Nicola said with a faint smile. "I want to hear how you're faring in your new role. I'm sure all of Grandfather's affairs keep you quite busy."

"There's much to learn, yes." Maryn wondered how much to share. Nicola had never been a confidante. "Grandfather's solicitors help immensely and a footman turned steward is proving quite able."

"I suppose you have little time for socializing."

"Being in mourning, no. But even out of it that's never been my forte."

"A pity, really. With your standing you could well attend Court functions in London and whatnot. Something I've always aspired to but alas my husband is a baron and I a mere baroness."

Maryn daren't tell her she'd agreed to the sale of the London townhouse. She stayed silent as a burst of girlish laughter sounded upstairs. Her spirits lifted. With no possibility of having children of her own—

"In my condition I rarely socialize either," Nicola continued. "Though I did have tea with Lady Lyon and her daughter recently. Do you know of them?"

Maryn shook her head. "There are several new families in Berwick, Mrs. Duncan told me. Are the Lyons among them?"

"Yes, they occupy Lyon Court on the Merse. Glaswegians, originally. Lady Lyon is rather sickly but her daughter, Miss

Ivory Lyon, is très belle. And it seems she's set her cap for none other than Mr. Hume."

Miss Ivory Lyon. The beauty she'd seen riding with Orin that day? All the breath left Maryn. She set down her teacup so quickly it rattled.

Nicola continued with a sort of gloating—or was it loathing? "'Tis rumored they're all but betrothed."

"Betrothed?"

Her sister's tone turned bitter. "Of all the suitors she could have, she's chosen a Hume. I'll never forgive him given he took Hershel's life. He's naught but a—"

"*Please.* Say no more." Maryn struggled for composure though Nicola's accusation was not new. "Orin Hume didn't take Hershel's life. I was in that sleigh with him whilst you were safely at home, far from the accident. Herschel, caught up in the moment—" Would she always recall the cold and the bells so clearly? "—challenged Mr. Hume to a regrettable race which he accepted. All was done in the spirit of fun during the wildest weather imaginable. None of us could have foreseen the heartrending consequences."

Nicola regarded her stonily. "A rather heated defense of a man who will always be nothing more than a murderous rogue to me."

The slur turned Maryn's stomach. "I hope you didn't belittle him to the Lyons."

"How dare you. Vulgar I am not." She expelled a breath. "For the life of me, I've never understood your willingness to forgive. Your acceptance of what happened. I believe it's the root of the rift between us."

Rift? She and Nicola had never been close. And much of that had to do with her sister's peevish nature. She'd turned more fractious since their parents' deaths and then Herschel's soon after. Misfortune visited them all. Why had it made her sister especially resentful?

"An accident, however tragic, is far more easily forgiven than an evil intended." Maryn's voice firmed though she still felt shaken. "As far as accepting what happened, what choice do I have?"

Nicola sipped her tea in sullen silence. Maryn regretted coming. How foolish she'd been to believe some sort of reconciliation between them could be reached. Her sister's vinegary attitude only doubled her angst. Just when Maryn could stand it no longer, into the chamber came the patter of little feet.

"Aunt Maryn!" A smiling Charlotte stood in the doorway, her joy transforming the tense drawing room. "Are you taking tea?"

"Indeed," Maryn said, relieved. "And I'm so delighted to see you."

Charlotte hurried across the chamber, her sisters following with less grace. Eugenie tripped over her gown and Penelope helped her to her feet, all the while their mother cautioning them to deport themselves like ladies.

Despite Nicola's protests, her youngest daughters climbed onto Maryn's lap while Lottie, as they called Charlotte, leaned into her. Remembering the sweets in her pocket, Maryn withdrew some candied orange peel in a square of embroidered linen. Beaming, they ate the treats as Lord Marchmont entered the room from a side door.

"Your Grace." His demeanor held the cordiality his wife's lacked. "Welcome to Redbraes."

"Good to see you, milord." Maryn felt an odd fondness—or was it sympathy?—for the mild-mannered gentleman whose health always seemed in question. Did the rule of a petticoat government at Redbraes have something to do with it? "Your daughters are even sweeter than I remember."

"They seem to change by the hour, truly." He chuckled, hands behind his back. "Pen has grown an inch since we last saw you."

"An inch!" Maryn rounded her eyes in exaggerated delight. "I don't suppose candied peel helps you grow?"

They giggled, chewing daintily, eyes on their mother as if she might scold them again.

Charlotte looked entreating. "May we come visit you, Aunt Mar—"

"*Your Grace*," Nicola insisted.

Maryn resisted the urge to roll her eyes. "You are welcome whenever you wish."

"I would like to come live with you," Charlotte said, finished with her sweet. "That way you'd have a wee daughter and Mama and Papa would still have Pen and 'Genie."

"Nonsense, Lottie," Nicola told her, pouring more tea. "Have your father take you three outside to play with your new puppy."

Penelope slipped off Maryn's lap and took her hand. "I want Auntie to see Nessie."

"The puppy?" Maryn asked.

Charlotte nodded. "She's a girl like us."

"I'd like nothing better," Maryn replied, standing and ignoring her sister's disapproval. "Puppies are one of God's best gifts."

"But God didn't give us Nessie. Papa did," Penelope said to her father's surprisingly robust laugh.

For the moment, Orin's near betrothal was pushed to the back of Maryn's mind.

Once in the coach on the way home, Maryn gave way to her somersaulting feelings. Glad she was that neither Rosemary nor

Alice accompanied her. She was alone with her emotions and damp handkerchief as she pondered Orin's future. Perhaps it wouldn't have cut so deeply had she heard it from someone else. Nicola's low regard of him seemed especially spiteful.

By the time her own gates came into view, she'd dried her eyes though she felt completely spent. Thankfully, her nieces proved the one bright thread in a grey afternoon. If only they could all pass regularly between Redbraes Castle and Lockhart Hall. She'd not had a feeling of family for so long she'd quite forgotten what it was like. And that was partly why she had declined the Countess of Wedderburn's invitation for tea. Being amid a whole, loving clan only magnified her own loss. Her own lack.

And now, knowing the only man she'd ever loved was to wed, she was doubly glad she'd declined. Time to let go and go on, as Orin had said. If ever there was a man made for a family, created to be a devoted husband and father, it was him. Perhaps Ivory Lyon was just the wife he needed. If so, she'd be especially blessed to marry a Hume.

If she herself couldn't have him as a husband, that didn't mean no one else could.

22

Wagons filled with crates of books were already arriving at Black Bull Street, so many that three of Wedderburn Castle's footmen had been borrowed to help unpack, dust, and shelve the gifted library. Though Orin's mind remained firmly on Maryn, always hoping she'd simply appear and surprise him, he was pleasantly distracted from their tenuous situation. The fact she'd given him the collection made his work more gratifying.

He picked out a particularly valuable book, its distinctive binding one of tooled leather. The vellum pages held Middle English and woodcut illustrations. He breathed in the musty scent and marveled at its excellent condition. Other rarities awaited, each unique and valuable.

Did Maryn realize the treasure trove she'd parted with?

He'd set up a desk in a side room with a view of the street and it was here Charis found him, head bent over a ledger like a lad at his studies. The front door opened and she swept in, a leather strap in hand with several brass bells attached. The festive sound resounded through the whole shop, sure to raise the most dour bibliophile's spirits.

"A shop must give a warm welcome." She stooped, her indigo skirts fanning out around her on the newly polished floor, and tied the jingling bells to the door handle. "Though I feared you might be reminded of a sleigh ... "

"Nay," he replied, shooting down the notion, and the melancholy memory with it. "A charming gift from my favorite niece."

"Your *only* niece," she parried, continuing their longstanding jest. "The Humes are quite good at begetting boys."

Chuckling, he stood and she kissed him on both cheeks. "Let me guess. You've come to visit the dressmaker again and hazarded me a second visit."

"Guilty." She sat in the windowseat, blocking his view of the busy street. "A society maiden's wardrobe is a work in progress."

"And when is our next function? I can't recall." He sat back down, nearly spilling a bottle of ink. One day his desk would have a semblance of order, but for now all was joyous chaos.

"A musical evening at Landreth Hall on Thursday next, followed by a dinner party at Duns Castle on Saturday." She began to rummage in her pocket. "But that's the least of my concerns at present."

He leaned back in his chair, wondering if a particularly precarious stack of books nearest her would topple. Reaching out, he secured them as she withdrew something from her purse.

"The papers have always adored you though this is of a decidedly unflattering nature."

He took the latest copy of *Tatler* from her. He'd not had time for any periodicals lately. Sunlight streamed upon the desktop and illuminated several inked lines, beginning with—

Bard of Britannia Disappears

He read on silently, glad only Charis was present to see his vexation. The footmen were busy upstairs.

Behold! A mirthful spectacle unfolds as Mr. Orin Hume, erstwhile Poet Laureate, hath forsaken his quill and laurels in exchange for that of Fortune Hunter. The King's countenance, though riddled with displeasure, finds relief in the appointment of Sir Walter Mayhew to the exalted position. Mr. Hume, wearied by the tierce of Canary wine that graced his laureateship, has traded London for Scotland in quest of a more opulent title—the coveted yet cursed Duchess of Fordyce.

Wheest!

Orin resisted the urge to fist the paper into a knot. Used to satire of the severest sort—though he never stooped to write it—he nevertheless felt such pillorying and lampooning a blow. Had Maryn read such nonsense? Better she hear it from him first.

"Of course, the pundit is anonymous, as is oft the case," Charis said, watching as he shrugged on his coat. "You're not riding to the printer in London, I'm sure, but Lockhart Hall."

"With an abject apology, aye."

A rather convenient way to continue your courting.

The voice lambasted him from within but he moved toward the door and lapsed into the broad Scots he used when aggravated. "I wouldna expect me for supper, scunnered as I am."

Charis followed him outside, the jingle of the bells now grating. "Well, dear uncle, I wish you every success in whatever it is you're about."

Maryn arranged the cut flowers in a vase atop her tidy desk. Dazzling light from her cabinet windows foretold noon, illuminating every hue of the heirloom roses. Butter yellow. Pale lavender. Rich apricot. Even a soft red, much like the rose Orin had picked for her at the gatehouse. The fragrance was intoxicating, filling the round chamber and driving out the stale tobacco scent. She'd banished Grandfather's Orinoco jar from the mantel, wondering if Orin took snuff like so many courtiers, but guessing he smoked a pipe like the laird, instead.

What did it matter? The thought needed banishing, too.

As she quashed it, hoofbeats alerted her to someone's coming. Tension coiled inside her at the thought of entertaining—or turning them away. She was hardly dressed for company. With Rosemary sick in bed with a cold, Maryn wore no stays, only a loose, belted sultana in rose silk. For once she wasn't wearing black.

When the rider reached the forecourt all her dread turned to an unwilling delight. *Orin.* Only he looked dark as a thundercloud. Had something gone awry? Was she to blame? Standing beside the half-arranged roses, she hastily pulled a stray thread from her sultana and pushed back a strand of hair.

A footman announced him and there Orin stood in the cabinet doorway, his intense expression on arrival relaxing. "Maryn."

"Thank you," she breathed, heartily tired of her title.

He removed his hat. "I'm sorry to arrive without warning."

"Your hurried hoofbeats were warning enough," she reassured him.

With a half-smile, he came into the room and admired the bouquet. "I never saw a rose in the past five years that I didn't think of you. Your gardens."

"Roses were always Mama's favorite, too."

"Unfortunately, I've not come to discuss roses but scandal."

Scandal? She gestured toward the damask sofa, flowers fleeing her thoughts.

Seated, they turned slightly toward each other, apology etched into his clear-cut features. "I've resigned as Poet Laureate. If you've read the latest newspapers or magazines you may already ken."

"Resigned?" She wasn't surprised. His leaving fit with what Nicola had told her. If he was to wed he would likely stay on in Berwickshire. With Miss Lyon ever in mind, she braced herself to hear his plans. "I thought Poet Laureate was a lifetime appointment."

"I'm the first to stand down. My life is here. London is behind me." He swallowed, clearly at sixes and sevens. "But my resignation makes me fodder for broadsheets and the like. Much as I want to spare you the ridiculous details, I've been labeled a fortune hunter and the press has named you as my prey."

"Prey?" Amusement turned to laughter, a surprisingly odd sound given she found so little mirthful of late. "Well, there's no one I'd rather be besmirched with than you."

"You're taking it better than I did."

She lifted her shoulders. "After the *Lockhart curse*, anything else pales in comparison."

His eyes still held regret. "I've only seen you a few times since returning to the Lowlands. For the life of me, I can't figure out who kens our association and made it public fodder."

"This too shall pass, as Grandfather used to say. The rags will report what they will and tomorrow it shall be about someone else."

"Aye, but it maddens me nonetheless. I care nothing for what they print about me but you are another matter. You are above such nonsense. Above reproach."

His protectiveness touched her. How good it was to be hemmed in with kindness and concern rather than feel vulnerable and alone. Wanting to divert him, she tugged at the bell pull. Mrs. Duncan brought raspberry shrub, made with honey from Lockhart Hall's aviary.

"So, I suppose this means you won't be attending the king's birthday ball," she said. "Leave that to the next Poet Laureate."

"I wish him well." His grimace told her much. "Five years at Court has cured me completely. 'Twas a soulless existence oftentimes."

"I can only imagine what goes on behind those gilded walls. But I also believe nothing we experience is ever wasted. Think of it as future literary inspiration."

"Inspiration, aye." His gratitude was palpable. "Life of late has taken a decidedly different turn. Because of you, I'm surrounded by such a quantity of books that it seems more like heaven on earth."

She smiled and looked down at the ripe raspberries atop her dwindling drink. "Remember when you used to read to me?"

"A voice deep as a velvet well, you used to say."

"That hasn't changed. Have you any recommendations?"

"A timely question. I've stowed away some books which will wait till you visit the shop." He set aside his empty glass. "Have *you* any recommendations?"

She smiled. "I'm rather taken with a certain play I just read in *The Gentleman's Magazine*."

"*Harlequin Restored* or *The Double Dealer?*"

"*Harlequin Restored*, soon to be staged at Drury Lane. The playwright must be deliriously happy."

"The playwright is only wondering if you've written anything in the last five years."

She bit her lip, wanting to spill everything, every success and frustration as in days of old. But to do so would make him her confidante. Usurp the lass he loved. She would say no more nor share her short-lived success in Edinburgh and then her subsequent humiliation of being lambasted as a garrulous female poet and playwright. Though she did wonder what he'd make of *The Queen Bee Chronicles*.

"I dabble," she said and took another sip. "And you deserve every accolade. I never doubted you would become a leading literary light when we were performing on garden benches."

"To be honest, I believe my life's work lies ahead of me. Establishing a literary presence in the Lowlands despite my critics."

"Critics are at every turn, no matter what one does. There are many who'll support you, myself foremost."

His gaze rose to the full shelves surrounding them. "I'm determined to press on regardless. Reading is a rare gift that needs to become commonplace."

"As Mr. Benjamin Franklin said, the person who deserves most pity is a lonesome one on a rainy day who doesn't know how to read."

"Yet few ken how and far fewer have books."

"Your bookshop and future lending library will help change that. As for myself, I've been pondering a teacher for the children of my tenants. There are a great many of an age to learn on Lockhart lands. They're often in the fields or laboring too young. Their time could be better spent with books, at least early on. Then they'd have more choices in later life."

"Agreed. I've spoken with the laird about the same and he's willing to listen."

"Great things start small." She strove to be an encouragement despite the enormity of it all. "And you've made a bold move with the bookshop."

"If I can catalogue the five thousand. I've completed half but keep getting distracted by those rare, ancient editions."

"A delightful dilemma." She imagined him sunk in those old pages, admiring the elaborate, hand-tooled bindings and colored leather. "If those books had come to me first they might have bypassed you altogether."

He smiled and met her eyes again.

Oh, that impossibly blue gaze … which still made a wash of her middle.

"Half have been shelved, too," he said.

"You sound too busy for any socializing. How is Lady Charis's season going?"

"Weel enough. The laird may announce her betrothal to Lord Lovell soon which would make us all breathe a sigh of relief."

"Oh? I'm so happy for her—for you all." Her mind began whirring.

Should she not offer her congratulations about his own betrothal? Or wait till such was announced? As much as the possibility pained her, not knowing the details chafed, too. But he said nothing about Miss Lyon. Amid the rose's perfume and the refreshing drinks she sensed a restlessness about him today. As if he was holding something back.

She ventured, "You're tired of minuets and small talk, then."

"Let's say I'm more comfortable in bookshops and gatehouses."

"As am I." Did Miss Lyon support his bibliophile bent? "I've nearly forgotten what it's like to attend a fête. I did so love to dance."

"What's to keep you from it once you're done with mourning?" He extended a hand. "What's to keep you from it now?"

She looked at him, her heart catching at the thought. Now, as in *right now*? In this very chamber? His gaze held hers in unmistakable invitation.

Torn, she looked away. "I...my injury. I've had to give up much I once loved, like the pianoforte and harp."

He nodded, compassion in his eyes. "But there's nae reason you canna dance again."

She looked to her left arm and hand, even now covered with a glove. "I suppose pride prevents me. Fear of what others might say. Their revulsion." Not to mention her own.

"Let me see, if you will," he said gently, reaching for her.

She all but recoiled. "Nay, Orin. I—" She stumbled over his name, not meaning to utter it but forgetting herself.

"Your injury doesn't disturb me, Maryn, just your reluctance to return to a full life."

A full life. He was right, of course. Her pride prevented her, much as she hated to admit it. And fear. Fear of what others thought or would invariably say.

"We had an arrangement once." He looked toward a window, his profile as heart-catching as ever. "Our families were in talks regarding our future. Do you remember?"

"I do recall it, yes." It had been, she wouldn't say, the sweetest years in hindsight. The world had been rose-hued before it became sable. Life had been full then. A title. Family. A noble house. Traditions. A young man who was her best friend with a promise of much more.

He continued, as if their estrangement had never happened. "I'd be less than honorable if I didn't express my desire for that arrangement to continue."

She blinked and all assumptions regarding Miss Lyon collapsed. Her throat seemed to close in answer. "But..."

"As a matter of honor, I ask you to consider it."

She swallowed as their eyes locked. "You mean... marriage?"

"Aye." He looked down at his hands, his signet ring bearing his initials on its bezel. "Marriage. A family. The life I hoped to have with you."

How his velvet voice wooed her. Reopened the door to the future she'd thought locked forever. She grasped for something to say, to push him—and her swelling tide of feelings—back. "As a matter of honor."

"Aye."

Ah, finally she understood. He felt obligated, then. Before he could form another alliance he needed to know that their former bond was irretrievably broken. For a few fleeting seconds the realization was akin to being hurled from the sleigh all over again. The room all but tilted and spun. She fought for breath as a crushing, bruising heaviness engulfed her.

She heard herself say, "Given that, my refusal would release you to move on... find happiness elsewhere."

He looked at her so intently it seemed he sensed her inward struggle. "Consider it, is all I ask."

"Nay...there's nothing left to consider. The facts remain."

She couldn't dismiss the medical reports, the multitude of doctors shaking their heads and concurring her injuries would likely prevent her from having children. So many dire, dark details. She couldn't tell him such delicate things.

"As I've said before, I'm not who I once was nor are you." Though her voice was soft there was steel beneath. "'Tis futile to try to go on as before."

He fisted his hands together. "I suppose you haven't found those letters. The missing ones. The ones you wrote to me."

She shook her head, looking toward the desk where his were still secreted. She'd considered asking Nicola about them but doing so might create another tempest she had no heart for. "They seem to have disappeared."

"I suppose that belongs in the past, too," he said and stood. "I've taken enough of your time today."

Nothing played across his stalwart face but she sensed her refusal wounded him more than it released or relieved him. And she hated she was the cause of it. Bewildered, she sat, combing over all they'd just said, trying to make sense of it once he'd left. When he rode away she hurriedly shut the door to her cabinet so none could witness her weeping.

23

*O*rin rode back to Wedderburn's gatehouse, barely aware of his surroundings. Had he gone too far? Pushed Maryn beyond her comfort—and thereby his? Uneasy as he was at the prospect, the simple fact she'd said his name heartened him. For a moment the Maryn he loved resurfaced and she'd let down her guard, let him in.

Before locking him out again.

Dust rose around him as he cantered down the main road to Duns. He wanted to return to the distracting disorder of the bookshop but his mind was so full of her he turned toward the privacy of the gatehouse to think things through instead.

Only that luxury might be denied him.

Charis was coming down the long drive from the castle on foot, purpose in her gait. To see him? He dismounted by the garden wall, handing the reins to a lad who'd return Septimus to the stables. When she drew close he saw that her eyes were red. From crying? The laird liked to call her a watering pot.

"Mightn't you have time for tea?" she asked, going ahead of him when he ushered her inside.

"Tea, aye," he echoed, thinking how satisfying it had been to enjoy a cold drink with Maryn despite their differences.

"Your gatehouse is cold even in summer though I do spy a low fire in the parlor." She pulled off her hat and discarded it on a chair. "Mama said you make a divine pot of tea though it tends to be a woman's domain, or at least associated with female tittle-tattle."

Again his thoughts veered to Maryn. "When you're without a lass..."

"I suppose you still have that coffee-mill Lady Mar—the duchess—once gave you?"

"At Hume House in London, aye. My belongings should be here soon, the mill with it." He took the steaming kettle from the hearth and filled a red stoneware teapot, choosing a porcelain cup for Charis. "But I sense you've not come to talk coffee or tea."

"I bring sad news." Her voice wavered much like Maryn's had done in the emotion of the moment. "Lord Lovell's— Marc's—father has died and he's to remain in England for now."

"I'm sincerely sorry to hear it." The dukedom, despite all its advantages, was a weighty matter. Lovell had never been close to his eccentric father. That sort of loss went hard on a man, mayhap harder, when somewhat estranged.

"Which means he'll be in mourning for a year or better and I'll never meet my future father-in-law."

He nearly groaned. He was sick to death of mourning. Maryn had had enough to last a lifetime and he wanted to see her in something other than sable though she'd surprised him by wearing color today.

He handed Charis the cup. "I'd hoped for a better start to your married life than a funeral."

"As did I. Of course I wrote him straightaway this morning to reassure him I'd be here to support him and wait on his timing to move forward. But Father said the marriage settlement is at a halt till mourning is done. He believes Marc needs time to assume his new title and all the responsibilities that come with it before matrimony. My reminder that he disregarded mourning to marry Mother doesn't seem to faze him."

"He's reluctant to part with you, remember." Orin sat in a Windsor chair, boots to the fire. "You're the last of his brood, so to speak."

"A year seems an eternity to wait." More downcast, Charis took a sip. "Suppose Marc changes his mind about me in that time. Finds someone else. An English lass nearer at hand who is better placed than a Lowland laird's daughter."

"If so, that tells a great deal about the man and your tie, aye?"

She looked at him entreatingly. "How does one ken for sure if what one has is lasting?"

"When ye ken, ye ken." He lapsed into Lowland speech again. Seeing that his pithy advice didn't assuage her, he spoke what he'd been mediating on of late. "Love is patient and kind. It doesna envy nor boast. It isna proud nor dishonoring. It isna self-seeking nor easily angered and keeps nae record of wrongs. Love doesna delight in evil but rejoices with the truth. It always protects, always trusts, always hopes, always perseveres."

"You quote first Corinthians."

"There's nae better measure."

She looked intently into the fire as if seeing her future there. "You seem to speak from experience."

Heat crawled up his neck but he said nothing. He was here to advise, not confess.

"I don't mean to pry, Uncle, but I'm not the only one who's been wondering the state of your heart."

He took a long, thoughtful sip of tea. "Meaning?"

She smiled, her reddened eyes less noticeable. "Miss Lyon has tasked me with finding out."

"She's a braisant lass. I'm surprised she doesna ask me herself."

"You missed the last social function so she's ensnared me. To your credit, you've not led her to believe she's the object of your affections. You've simply been gentlemanly. Her own hopes fuel her persistence."

"She'll soon move on. The harvest is always richer in another man's field."

She held out her empty cup and he refilled it. "Since I owe you the respect due an uncle, I'll not press you further."

"Some matters are better left alone."

"Very well. Are you still squiring me to the musical evening at Landreth Hall?"

"Count on it." Though he was in no mood for more society without Maryn. Lately anything without her seemed increasingly lacking, including this abode. He couldn't rid his mind of a life with her. Of children. Life and laughter. He wanted to show her joy and health could be had. Even dancing.

He wanted to make her smile again.

The news came at night. Once the gloaming signaled blessed bedtime and sweet dreams but since Herschel's loss, Maryn had developed a dread of the dark and what it might bring. Bad news always seemed to visit in the wee small hours. And now...

Mrs. Duncan woke her. "Your Grace, a servant has come bearing a message from Redbraes. Your sister's lying in is at hand and the doctor despairs of her very life."

The housekeeper's alarmed words shook off the last vestiges of sleep. Maryn began dressing hurriedly with the help of a roused Rosemary as word was sent to the stables to ready a coach to depart. Childbirth was always fraught with great risk. She'd assumed with three healthy births that Nicola would have no woes with the next. She so wanted a son and heir.

The midnight journey across the Lowlands seemed endless, further blackened by speculations and fears. Rain sent the coach wheels sliding on muddy corners and Rosemary crying out in alarm. What if they arrived too late? What if it was a false alarm? Would the babe survive?

No more mourning, Lord. Please.

Once there, Maryn was shown into the anteroom of the birthing chamber. Ladykirk's minister and two nurses were also present, the low drone of their voices like the hum of summer's bees. Also on hand was the accoucheur from Edinburgh, the male-midwife who'd been present at Nicola's other births.

Face to face with her sister, Maryn realized the situation was grave. The strained feeling in the room—Nicola's obvious distress and exhaustion—seemed to shout danger.

Maryn turned to Lord Marchmont, wanting to do more than wring her hands. "Can I be of any help?"

Relief crossed his wan face. "Please go see about the girls. Eugenie was restive earlier and crying. Their nurse is needed here."

A maid ushered her down a hall where wall sconces lit their way to a large nursery. Eugenie had stopped her crying but sat in her crib, tears shining in the candlelight. She lifted her arms to Maryn. But could she pick her up? Summoning all her strength, she did so clumsily if safely then sat in a near chair to better balance her youngest niece on her lap.

Instinct had her doing as her own mother had done, rocking and singing a nearly forgotten lullaby. In the adjoining room were Charlotte and Penelope in their more grown-up beds, sleeping soundly.

Maryn breathed more easily in this quiet, rose-pink room, relieved to be away from Nicola's suffering. Never had she attended a birth nor wanted to. For a moment grief gave way to relief given she'd been told she might never conceive or carry a child. Childbirth was not for the faint-hearted.

As the clock crept toward dawn, Eugenie slept in her lap. Maryn's own back and arm ached at this unexpected but welcome burden nestled against her. She sat and prayed, even dozed, till a newborn's cry jerked her awake. Surely the sound of a healthy babe.

Footsteps in the hall ensued. The nursery door came open. Lord Marchmont stood there and one look at his haggard face told her everything.

Nicola had not survived the ordeal. But the babe had.

With his help, she returned Eugenie to her crib and covered her with a blanket, balking at what awaited. Lord Marchmont led her back to the birthing chamber where Nicola had been laid out in a fresh nightgown, her hands folded on her chest. A maid opened a window as morning snuck past the shutters.

"A son," Lord Marchmont choked out.

Maryn looked at the infant in the nurse's arms, still squalling and very much alive, his mother gone. She could hardly come to terms with it, stunned past speech when she was handed the newborn.

"He mustn't be called Herschel." Lord Marchmont was more decisive than she'd ever seen him. "It seems a bad omen. I want him named after your father."

"Haddon?" Who was she to argue with a stricken widower?

He nodded and went on woodenly, "She's written a farewell letter…updated her will, as many expectant mothers do. And she expressly stated she wants our children to be brought up by you."

24

As much as Orin enjoyed music, the evening at Landreth Hall felt interminable. Several guests performed with the hired musicians, including Miss Lyon on the pianoforte. For the hundredth time that night, his mind returned to Maryn. It made him half crabbit that she was absent. Maryn played the pianoforte and harp, or once did. She should be here beside him, enjoying the music if not entertaining.

A female soloist took center stage, her swelling soprano reminding him of a performance long ago in London. Beside him, Charis wore a faraway look, no doubt missing Lovell and wondering about their future. When the piece ended, his niece left his side to speak with friends while he discussed his bookshop's opening and rumblings of a new Jacobite Rising with a few gentlemen from Duns. Miss Lyon appeared, making her way to his side when the men went in search of punch.

"You seem rather preoccupied tonight, Mr. Hume." She flicked her fan open, wafting it about so vigorously he felt its wind. "Perhaps you're as shocked as I about the ill news."

News? Orin felt in the dark and on guard all at once.

"Just now I learned from Lady Blackadder that another tragedy has befallen Berwick. It seems the Lockhart curse has struck again."

Maryn? His every nerve turned taut. "What means you?"

"Not long ago Mother and I had tea at Redbraes Castle with Lady Marchmont. It seems she died in childbirth yestreen leaving her family reeling. The babe lives but..."

Nicola? He hadn't even known she was expecting. Maryn hadn't mentioned it but she rarely talked about family, even her own sister. He did ken Lord Marchmont wasn't in the best health but couldn't recall how many children they had.

Miss Lyon was studying him in a way he could only call dissecting. "I remember you once had close ties to the Lockhart family."

Once cut coldly. Colder still was the realization that Maryn had been dealt another death on the heels of her grandfather's passing. "I'm most acquainted with the late baroness's sister."

"Ah, yes. A failed marriage settlement of some sort, 'tis said. And now, lo and behold, she's a duchess, removed from your realm completely. Perhaps if you'd accepted that baronetcy..."

He listened but his mind couldn't latch hold of the details. All that mattered was that Maryn was safe. Sound. But no doubt shattered over another loss.

"Her Grace is a recluse, I understand," she continued though her fan had stilled. "Unable to return to society due to her injuries from that unfortunate accident you were a part of."

Orin suspected Nicola had blamed him publicly for Herschel's death as well. She'd always held him responsible, God rest her troubled soul. For now, he'd had enough of Miss Lyon and her meddling. To his relief, the soloist approached, her smile resurrecting a past meeting.

"Mr. Hume, imagine seeing you again," she began, "after our less than illustrious beginning in London."

"Miss Hazel Robson." He gave a slight bow, remembering the incident and wanting to put her at ease. "A genuine pleasure whether here or there."

"You continue very courtly, sir. I still owe you a debt of gratitude for coming to my rescue."

At this, Miss Lyon took her leave as Orin and Miss Robson moved toward a French door.

"That summer was particularly stifling and His Majesty refused to open any windows if memory serves." Orin gestured outside, her fainting firmly in mind. "I'm in need of some fresh air myself."

She nodded. "Our thoughts align though I do find Scottish summers far more comfortable than those in the city."

They continued down wide steps onto a lantern-lit walkway that skirted a pond. Twin swans glided by, their plumage silvery beneath a full moon. A few other couples walked about, their murmurings threading through the sultry stillness.

"Are you here in the Lowlands long?" Orin asked, eyes on the swans even as his thoughts swung to Lockhart Hall.

"'Till Christmas. My voice needs a rest and my aunt lives in Polwarth. She's invited me to stay with her there."

"Not far then." He couldn't help but add, *"At Polwarth on the Green, if you'll meet me in the morn, where lads and lasses do convene, to dance around the thorn."*

"My aunt has quoted that same old rhyme," she said with a smile, pausing to remove a pebble from her slipper. "I find Polwarth—the Merse—especially lovely right now."

"You've come at a good time. Midsummer is when the Lowlands are at their best."

"I heard you're opening a bookshop. I shall do some reading while here and must visit Duns."

"Visit, aye. You'll be among our first customers."

They started up the steps to return to the house, his hand on her sleeve to steady her. Her blondeness was in direct contrast to Maryn's blue-black. Of the same height, Maryn was not the sylph this lass was. Miss Robson looked almost fairy-like, may-hap frail.

When they reentered the house, Orin checked the urge to consult his watch. A glass of punch and several business-related questions later, he bided his time till Charis stifled a yawn and returned to his side.

"I see you've renewed your acquaintance with the angelic-voiced, very agreeable Miss Robson," she said conspiratorially. "A much more suitable match than Miss Ivory Lyon...if I were to be accused of matchmaking, that is."

With a half-hearted chuckle, Orin escorted her from the house to the waiting carriage. "I make nae such accusation but your high praise is duly noted."

Back in the gatehouse, Orin found himself reading till midnight. Or trying to. He'd brought home a few compelling books from the bookshop but Maryn's bereavement intruded, and he wondered her possible reaction to her sister's death. With no family to console or comfort, she would forge ahead alone with her grief. He didn't believe in the Lockhart curse but this latest tragedy confirmed the family was indeed marked by extraordinary grief.

"I'm shocked and heartbroken for them, especially Maryn," Charis had said on their return home. "How much tragedy can one family endure? There's no end to their mourning."

Rising from his chair, he set the book aside and wandered outside to the walled garden. Drenched in moonlight, it had a ghostly aspect that fit his mood. Turmoil vied with melancholy as he debated his next step.

Should he go to Maryn or merely send her a note of condolence?

She'd made it abundantly clear about his company.

I'm not who I once was nor are you. 'Tis futile to try to go on as before.

Wasn't that his answer to his pursuit of her, then? She clearly wanted no part of it. Add to that the burn of Miss Lyon's forthright words and there was abundant proof it was futile to have any hope of rekindling their relationship.

A failed marriage settlement of some sort ... and now, lo and behold, she's a duchess, removed from your realm completely.

Her words were driven by spite, the small-mindedness of a woman thwarted. But they still merited unraveling. True, the marriage settlement between him and Maryn had failed because of the tragedy. Once they had been nearly inseparable, though now he wondered if his own romantic nature colored their tie as having been more than it was.

Mayhap the Almighty was even using the disagreeable Miss Lyon to shine truth on his situation lest he become mired in it. It might even be that Miss Robson was not happenstance either. Given that, this seemed a chance to consider what was before him, forsake the complicated past, and forge a different sort of future.

But could he?

He needed counsel, but Lovell was gone. The laird was often embarrassingly blunt, the countess ever obliging, and Charis too inquisitive. He had few confidantes here as he'd lived in London so long—and even his peers in the city weren't always trusted nor wise.

He walked the perimeter of the knot garden, fragrant even at night, bypassing the cool spray of the fountain till he came to the opening in the stone wall. His hand sought the rough stone even as he felt a beat of hope that a letter would rest there, waiting. But the space was empty.

Empty as his heart.

25

*H*ow life could turn like a Highland road. Maryn felt at the edge of another cliff, unsure of herself and her destination. Frayed and frightened and out of her depth. A sennight had passed since Nicola's burial. Condolence letters were pouring in from across Berwickshire and beyond though she only cared for one. Orin's came in his striking Copperplate hand. Though terse, she sensed the beat of strong emotion beneath. She kept the note in her pocket as if somehow it could bolster her.

> *Dearest Maryn,*
>
> *I have no words to convey the depth of my sorrow for what is another untimely loss. I can only offer you my thoughts, prayers, and assistance for whatever you need should you need such.*
>
> *Your entire,*
Orin Hume

Maryn kept to her cabinet, overwhelmed with estate business and communications with her Edinburgh solicitors amid her grief. And today was the day when life as she knew it turned on end all over again.

"Your Grace..." Mrs. Duncan, ever composed, seemed somewhat shaken herself as she stood in the tiled hall at the foot of the staircase. "We're finally ready for the arrival of your wee nieces and nephew. The nursery has been aired, cleaned, and organized, along with the adjoining upstairs rooms needed by the nurses. If you'd like to take a look."

"I trust your preparations completely." Maryn expressed her thanks to the woman who continued to serve them unfailingly. "I admit to being overwhelmed by all this. I never thought to marry nor be a mother."

"Four bairns all at once are a challenge, especially when one is a newborn, though we shall have plenty of help from the new servants."

The wet nurse foremost, Maryn didn't say. How ironic that her wish to spend time with her nieces had come to this. Nicola's will had expressly stated the children be brought up at Lockhart Hall under her care and supervision, a shock that couldn't be second-guessed or denied.

"I do fret so about poor Lord Marchmont." Mrs. Duncan's face grew pinched with concern. "An ill and now grieving widower."

"I worry, too. His doctors have advised him to seek a warmer climate to ease his lung ailment. He's departing to the south of France as soon as the children and staff are settled."

"Wise, mayhap. I do wish him a speedy return to health." Mrs. Duncan looked toward the front door where a footman stood. Did she hear the children's approach? "'Tis not uncommon for wee ones to be reared by servants though I suspect you have in mind a different sort of arrangement."

"I shall try my best to mother them as my dear mother mothered me." Lately all sorts of memories were resurfacing of her own unusual childhood. Though their father had been somewhat distant, even absent as so many aristocrats were, their mother had not. From what Lord Marchmont had told her, Nicola had taken after their father in terms of child-rearing though he wished otherwise.

"A pearl of great price, your mother. God rest her gracious soul." Taking a handkerchief from her pocket, Mrs. Duncan dried her eyes. "And how pleased she would be that you've placed her portrait above the mantel in your cabinet."

"Let it be a reminder to me of her legacy of love and compassion." Maryn would keep her memory alive by telling her nieces about her. "How she would rejoice in her beautiful grandchildren."

Even as she finished the sentence a commotion in the forecourt brought her to her feet. Lord Marchmont's coach had arrived with not one but two baggage wagons while he himself rode a bay horse. Maryn braced herself for the noise and bustle to come.

Lord, I am out of my depth. Yet 'tis You Who have brought me to this moment. And I trust in Your equipping and provision. Amen.

Lord Marchmont appeared first, looking not only wan but blatantly apologetic. "I fear we descend on you like a whirlwind, Your Grace."

"Welcome, whirlwind or not. All is ready. Your own well-being is of paramount importance to me. And you shall have no worries at all on account of your children. I vouchsafe they shall be as happy and healthy as I can make them here at Lockhart Hall."

"I have no concerns in that regard, just profound thanks." He watched as a nurse appeared bearing a bundle. "I must warn you that my heir doesn't seem to sleep nor ken when his appetite is sated."

"Then I'm all the more thankful for the additional help you've provided," Maryn reassured him, moved by his obvious struggle. "We've made every arrangement for everyone's continued comfort here."

"Leave-takings are always my undoing so I will just depart without fuss. I have another stop to make before I reach the coast by nightfall, or so I hope." With a hasty adieu, he bowed as his daughters cleared the front steps, stopping long enough to embrace them.

Into the hall poured Penelope, Charlotte, and Eugenie in a high state of excitement despite their family upheaval, their pup, Nessie, on their heels. Nurse followed after them, a stout, middle-aged Duns woman who seemed wreathed in smiles and impervious to tantrums and tears. She dropped a curtsey as the girls left her side and swarmed round Maryn's colorful chintz petticoats. For now she'd set aside her mourning garments, at least when at home. The children needed no reminder of their recent loss.

"Ah, at last, wee ones." Maryn smiled and started up the stairs, taking the youngest in hand.

Charlotte looked up at her with a tentative smile. "Papa says you are to watch over us now that Mama is in heaven. You will be our mama on earth."

"Your papa is right. I'm blessed indeed. I've always wanted a daughter—and now I have three."

"And a wee lad who likes to howl," Pen said as she scooped up the puppy. "Nessie is better behaved."

"And you, Miss Eugenie?" Maryn looked down at her youngest niece who was taking the stairs slowly. "What do you think of your new brother, Haddon?"

"He's bonny," she echoed shyly, concentrating on her steps.

"Papa says I am to help you all I can while he's away. He said he will be gone for a long time but after a while he will visit us." Charlotte spoke with all the gravity of the eldest, Nicola firmly stamped on her features. "I think we shall like living here with you. I want to see the gardens again."

"I've had the old playhouse of mine and your mother's remade for you near the wood." Maryn had taken a special joy in overseeing that project. "Your father has sent all your play-pretties over to your new rooms here in hopes you'll feel more at home. For now, a milk tea awaits and since I'm rather ravenous I'll sit down with you myself."

"My tummy is growling," Pen said, giggling as Nessie licked her cheek. "I do hope you have tarts. Raspberry tarts are my favorite."

"Raspberry *and* lemon. We shall have a feast." Maryn welcomed them into the nursery where a table was laid with miniature dishes. "And then we shall go outside for fresh air."

"He's a bit of an armful, Yer Grace," Nurse said as she handed Maryn her nephew later that afternoon. "I'll be in the nursery unpacking the children's belongings should ye need me."

Maryn thanked her, standing in her cabinet, where light illuminated her hefty nephew's every curve and dimple. Clad in a simple linen gown and cap, Haddon slept, looking so like Herschel that Maryn marveled. The dark hair and long-lashed eyes. A braw bairn with tiny features promising a strapping lad in time.

Or would the Lockhart curse continue?

A chill hugged her spine as snugly as her stays. Nay, she did not believe in curses, only blessings. And holding this babe convinced her that there was healing to be had even amid heartache. The wee lamb embroidered on his blanket brought to mind a beloved verse.

He shall feed his flock like a shepherd: he shall gather the lambs with his arm, and carry them in his bosom, and shall gently lead those that are with young.

She would trust in that heavensent promise one moment at a time.

26

Inside his office on Black Bull Street, Orin attended to the day's business. A prodigious amount of work had been required before opening, including replacing a broken shop window the sheriff suspected was malicious. Again, Orin was reminded not everyone approved of his endeavors, however well intentioned.

Today the late summer sun was shining and the shop's long frontage was flanked by multi-paned Crown bullion glass. The new trade sign with its black lettering and scrolled skirt had been mounted and now hung from its wrought-iron armature, swinging slightly in a Lowland wind, beckoning one and all.

Wedderburn Books.

Beneath this was a painted image of a quill and a Bible. And so Orin Hume joined the ranks of booksellers across Britain with his shelves of catalogued books, stationary supplies, ink and the continual jingle of Charis's bells at the door alerting him to those who came to trade or simply gawk.

"Sir, a gentleman is here to see ye." The Duns lad he'd hired stood in the doorway of his office, halting his letter to a London printer.

"Send him in then."

Orin stood as a tall, lanky man in black approached, hat in hand. Lord Marchmont? "My apologies, sir, for the unexpected visit."

"None needed, milord." Orin gestured to a chair. Marchmont looked wearied. Harried. And with good reason. "Might I offer you a dram?"

"Aye, most welcome. I've a long journey ahead."

Concerned, Orin poured him whisky. "My sincerest apologies for your loss."

"Thank you." Sitting, Marchmont reached for the glass. "I'm still in shock yet hopeful time in the south of France restores my health if not my spirits. But that's not what brings me to your door." He took a drink, his hand unsteady. "I've gone through my late wife's belongings recently and discovered letters meant for you that somehow ended up in her possession."

Orin felt a beat of disbelief as he poured himself a drink. "Letters?"

"Aye, not written by my wife but her sister, now Duchess of Fordyce." Reaching into his weskit, he retrieved a stack and handed it across the desk. "They come with an apology. I fail to understand why she had them. Apparently there was some sort of argument between her and her grandfather about the correspondence years ago. I can only guess she somehow intercepted the letters and kept them."

Orin took them and did a quick count. Eight? In a trice they became the most precious thing in his possession. To Nicola's credit, the seals were intact, thus she hadn't read any, just hoarded them. "I'm grateful to have them."

"I recall there was some understanding between you and my sister-in-law at one time." He paused to cough. "And I have reason to believe my late wife wanted to put an end to that for unknown reasons when it wasn't her place to do so."

Orin swallowed. That poignant heaviness mixed with longing when he thought of Maryn stole over him again. He didn't ken what to say. Mayhap it wasn't his place to say anything. Especially not rail against a dead woman.

"I leave you now feeling relieved though I don't understand why." Marchmont stood and thanked him for the drink. "And I wish you every success here on Black Bull Street."

Once he left the shop, Orin went to a corner safe and stored the letters away, his carefully ordered day unraveling. What had Maryn penned back then in the shadow of the tragedy? He needed privacy away from the shop to find out but the door's bells alerted him to more customers on the heels of Lord Marchmont's exit.

Miss Hazel Robson and her aunt?

They greeted him, exclaiming with pleasure as they looked about. Introductions were made and Orin found the middle-aged Mrs. Robson to be remarkably well read.

"I do so enjoy literature of all sorts," Mrs. Robson said. "Lately I've finished *Beauty and the Beast* by Barbot de Villeneuve and *Sinners in the Hands of an Angry God* by Jonathan Edwards."

"Aunt Eleanor's reading tastes are quite varied as you can see," Miss Robson teased.

"And you?" Orin asked her, showing them upstairs. "What is your preference?"

"Novels," she said, gravitating toward a window-lit corner where those were shelved. "And you seem to have a fine selection."

Orin felt both pride and pleasure at her appreciation. "We have more books arriving every day. If you don't see what you fancy, I can order from Edinburgh or London."

She selected a copy of *Robinson Crusoe*, his personal preference. Might they have common ground? Their eyes met briefly before he looked away, turning his attention to another novel she might like.

"I'm most drawn to romantic stories." She opened the book and read a random line. Her speaking voice was as lovely as her singing voice. "*For sudden joys, like griefs, confound at first.*"

Aye, Orin thought, riven by both.

Orin vowed to wait till he returned to the privacy of Wedderburn's gatehouse to open the first of Maryn's letters. But the day's delays had him chafing against the clock that seemed to have frozen on the bookshop wall. Locking up, he eyed the new glass windows and uttered a prayer for his property's protection. Perhaps even vandals would one day learn to read and rue their mischief.

Finally, in the gloaming, he rode home. *Home.* The gatehouse had become more a home than Hume House in London ever had. Arriving at the castle, he left Septimus at the stables before giving the steward a book he'd inquired about, finally free to walk down the dusty drive, unsure if he'd return for supper. His stomach clenched as he pondered the letters he carried.

But first, his usual routines needed observing. He washed up at the washstand in his bedchamber and changed into a freshly laundered sark. Returning downstairs, he lit a pewter sconce. The mellowing whisky with Marchmont had long since worn off and his mind felt razor sharp. Laying the letters out atop a table, he hesitated. Someone—Maryn?—had numbered them in the corners. Or was it Nicola's doing? He needn't guess the order to read them.

Thunderstruck by the turn of events, he hesitated as the significance of the moment settled. With a swipe of his thumb he broke the first seal and all but held his breath.

Dearest Orin,

I have finally come to my senses and worse than my injuries is your absence. The accident, tragic though it was, seems to have brought clarity about a great many things, namely my regard of you. It is as Jean de La Bruyere said. "Love seizes us suddenly, without giving warning, and our disposition or our weakness

*favors the surprise; one look, one glance, from the fair fixes and
determines us."*

*You once said the sweetest of all sounds is the voice of a woman
beloved. I can add to that in reverse. The sweetest of all sounds
is your voice, spoken to me, near at hand. Since I last saw you
I love you a hundredfold more than I did when I seemed to be
half-asleep, never fully realizing the hard parting that would come
to us, all that you mean to me, and the depth of my feeling for
you. Can our hearts be one and the same? Please write to me as
soon as you are able. I await your response like my next breath.*

Ever thine,
Maryn

The candlelight flickered and he let go of the paper. It fluttered to the tabletop like a broken-winged moth. His heart had
picked up as though he'd run to the castle and back. A hard,
thudding beat that seemed to demand he do something. The
next letter was dated soon after the first and was a tad longer.
Several lines leapt out at him.

*You engross me so completely that I scarce think of anything else.
Not only do you occupy my daily thoughts but by night you
invade my sleep. I meet you in my dreams and dread waking for
it is to lose you all over again.*

Never doubt my fervent affection for you.

He read on, beguiled. Ensnared all over again. Her letters
pulsed with thinly veiled passion and then, by the last, became
threaded with a sadness that he had not written her back.

Only he had.

He nearly ground his teeth in frustration. How different
life would look had there been no tragedy, no separation, no
thwarted letters.

What now?

He rode to Lockhart Hall the next day. Unannounced. Unsure of his reception.

"Mr. Hume, do come in." Mrs. Duncan, at least, seemed happy to see him. "I'll show you to the garden. Her Grace is there now with the children."

Children? He could hear distant voices. Laughter. A bairn's cry rent the tiled hall. What? He looked upwards in the direction of the sound.

"Much has changed since you were last here," she said over her shoulder as she led him through a wainscoted corridor.

"My hope is Her Grace hasn't wed," he murmured to her answering chuckle.

"I'd best let her ladyship do any explaining, sir."

Outside, he stood, half-hidden by an arbor overlooking a side lawn as Mrs. Duncan excused herself. The Duchess of Fordyce was at a distance, looking like the Maryn of old in a bright yellow gown. Smiling, even laughing, and playing a game. On the grass was a rectangular, chalked grid. Hopscotch? Several little lasses—his heart caught at the endearing sight—were jumping and bending to retrieve colorful, tossed toys.

Hollowness gnawed at him alongside an addling confusion. He didn't ken who these bairns were. Maryn hadn't confided in him. It further underscored their divide. Whoever they were, they brought her a great deal of pleasure. He'd not seen that carefree smile nor heard her laugh since Herschel was alive.

The four of them were unaware of him and so he sat on the arbor seat, unwilling to interrupt their game. Only the dog, as if tired of being underfoot, ambled toward him. He bent and ran a hand over the spaniel's silky fur before it returned to the game.

They'd still not noticed him, caught up in the joyous moment and the late summer sunshine and their playing, wholly absorbed in the moment as only bairns could be.

As minutes ticked past a severe poignancy knifed him. This might have been his and Maryn's home. Their children. A complete, happy family unmarred by absence and loss.

Why hadn't he confessed his love for her when he'd broached marriage again as a matter of honor? Why hadn't he told her outright the feelings he'd once had for her he had for her still? That she was his first thought and his last, bookending the day like the tomes in his shop. That every woman he met also met her as their measure. He supposed his pride had prevented outright honesty. He'd barely stayed stoic when she'd rebuffed him.

Her letters now seemed to burn a hole against his chest, tucked inside his waistcoat. From a woman who no longer wanted him. Who'd said the same outright. And here he was all but groveling at a distance, watching her unawares. A sick certainty of how this would end clawed at him. There was still time to leave with a shred of dignity and decency before he made a fool of himself.

Or a fool of them both.

27

Winded yet refreshed, Maryn returned inside with her nieces for their lie down. Nurse called for the three to come to the nursery and wash hands, their flushed faces reflecting their pleasure from being outside. Once they'd rested they'd have a milk tea as was their custom. Though Lockhart Hall had been their home only briefly, a comfortable routine was already taking hold, adding delight and color to their days.

Straw hat in hand, Maryn watched them scurry upstairs, their grass-stained petticoats resembling flowers in hues of rose, lilac, and buttercup. Thank heavens children were excused from wearing mourning. Oddly enough, the girls rarely asked about their parents. They seemed content with the present and Maryn sought to make it as snug and secure as she could.

She enjoyed overseeing the nursery immensely. The toys and games. The clothes and shoes and tiny caps. The whimsy of it all. Bending down, she retrieved Eugenie's lost slipper on the stairs. The girls' chatter nearly snuffed the babe's crying from his end of the nursery. She started up the steps to go to him then paused, certain it was his wet nurse he wanted. Haddon was thriving on a great deal of nestling and milk. At least she could help with the nestling part.

"Your Grace..." Mrs. Duncan's voice turned her round.

Something about supper, she supposed. The housekeeper was punctilious about the day's menu.

"Mr. Hume was just here. Did you see him?"

Maryn stared at her blankly. "Mr. Hume? I—nay."

"I showed him to the side lawn where you were playing with your nieces."

Had she overlooked him? Retracing her steps, Maryn hastened outside, hope making her heart ache then nearly break to find the side lawn empty. Why had he come? Had he stood here watching her and the girls? What made him leave instead?

A sennight passed. Seven days in which Maryn watched and waited, hoped and prayed Orin would return and solve the mystery of his appearing. She paced the nursery on the following Monday, Haddon in arms. Just fed, he looked up at her with wide blue eyes, content and quiet, a momentary salve to her restless heart. And hers to raise.

But didn't a boy need a father near at hand?

Lord Marchmont might, in truth, never return to Scotland from France. At least she could provide for her nephew and nieces as best she could and pray for her brother-in-law's recovery. But if he didn't recover?

She continued to pace with Haddon who was soon lulled to sleep by her back-and-forth motion. Outside the day beckoned. A bright, September afternoon that held the abundance of autumn. Years ago, she and Orin would go foraging for mushrooms and berries or ride about in the pony cart on afternoons like these.

Returning Haddon to his crib as gently as she could, Maryn tucked in his blanket lest he be cold. For a moment she stood watching him, feeling every inch the mother. Awed. Protective. Loathe to leave his side.

Once downstairs again, she tried to attend to some publishing business in her cabinet. The girls were in their part of the nursery, well away from their sleeping brother. She could hear their high, happy voices as they played with their dolls, Nurse supervising.

Lately, Charlotte had shown an interest in stitching and so Maryn had ordered her a sewing kit from Edinburgh. Now seven, she would soon need schooling, necessitating a governess be found. Taking up a quill, Maryn composed an advertisement for the Edinburgh newspapers.

Wanted, a female tutor of genteel manners, an informed mind, and capable of teaching different kinds of needle-works. Also necessary that she should translate and speak French.

That done, she set it aside, her thoughts veering to Orin again.

Always Orin. Perhaps if she returned to the cottage she could find a measure of peace.

"Please prepare the chaise," she told a footman, summoning Rosemary besides.

In a half hour they were raising the dust of the road, bypassing Thistle cottage altogether. What had Orin told her? She'd pondered it ever since she'd last seen him.

Your injury doesn't disturb me, Maryn, just your reluctance to return to a full life.

"Och, Yer Grace!" Rosemary looked askance at her as she handled the reins. "Did I hear ye right when ye said Duns instead?"

"Duns, indeed," Maryn said, eagerness vying with trepidation. "The bookseller on Black Bull Street."

Time to run toward life rather than away from it.

"Verra weel." Rosemary tried not to smile but Maryn knew her too well and detected it. "Ye've nae been to Duns in an age."

"You may as well ken that I have business with Mr. Hume," she confessed.

"I dinna doubt it." Her maid's smile could no longer be contained. "Might we have time for the dressmaker besides? I have my heart set on a bit o' ribbon or lace."

"Of course. Why don't you go there whilst I visit the bookshop?"

"Have ye need of anything yerself?"

"Smelling salts," Maryn said wryly, having forgotten her vinaigrette. "Hartshorn should do."

"Ooh, aye. Mr. Hume makes one tapsalteerie, he does." Chuckling, Rosemary slowed the chaise as they passed a wagon. "Pardon me for saying so. I canna speak for the both of us, though if I could I'd say ye feel the same."

Maryn almost laughed. All those years with Rosemary attending her had bred an unusual familiarity between mistress and servant but it was what it was. Rosemary had been, for a long time, more friend.

Duns rose up in the distance, looking larger than Maryn remembered—and twice as daunting. Steeling herself lest she meet anyone who might recognize her, she took note of the buildings, old and new. Duns market, when all of Berwickshire descended, was held weekly but not today. At least she'd skirted that. Perhaps soon she'd not feel so anxious, so aware of her wound.

As they turned down Black Bull Street, Wedderburn Books was easily distinguished by its new trade sign and shining bow-fronted windows. Several horses and conveyances waited outside. An encouraging sight. Maryn wanted Orin not only to realize his dream but have it be the start of more successes. And to think she'd played some part in it all with her donation of the library collection and sale of the building.

She left the chaise, smoothing her sable petticoats at the entrance to the shop. Would its owner even be there? A clerk opened the door with a slight bow, and as she stepped inside, the aroma of countless books enfolded her. Several men perused the shelves—and a few women. One in particular. Only she wasn't perusing the shelves but the bookseller himself. Immediately Maryn regretted coming. Had she interrupted a tete-a-tete?

Miss Ivory Lyon was even lovelier than expected since she'd not gotten a good look at her on horseback that disturbing day. Now she turned toward Maryn with a questioning half-smile, her eyes communicating that she rued the interruption.

"Your Grace." Orin gave a slight bow that was as unnecessary as it was gallant. "Welcome to Wedderburn Books."

"I'm glad to see it busy," she said, smiling at Miss Lyon if only to stop herself from looking at him. "Is that coffee I detect?"

"Aye, a bookshop without it seems half crime," he replied, "though lately I'm in danger of turning this place into *Hume's Coffeehouse* instead. Would you care for a cup?"

"I would, indeed," she said, turning in a circle to better see the bookshop from all angles. "As the composer, Mr. Bach, has said, "'Ah! How sweet coffee tastes! Lovelier than a thousand kisses, sweeter far than muscatel wine! I must have coffee...'"

When she circled back to him and looked him fully in the face she gasped. He met her gaze unflinchingly though his left eye sagged shut. Purplish-black bruises mottled his bewhiskered jaw and the split to his lip made her wince. But it was the vicious slash below his right eye that most worried her.

A furious fear gripped her, its talons sharp. She'd never considered losing him before. His own mortality had been constant, never in question. Until now—

"Orry, what's been done to you?" Her heartfelt words seemed to echo to the shop's four corners.

"I was late coming home from here one night when a few vagabonds decided to steal my horse and berate me about my books." A trace of amusement lifted his voice. "The laird and sheriff soon rounded them up and sent them to the Edinburgh Tolbooth. Septimus was returned unharmed."

Overcome, she could only reach out and clasp his hand in silent support when what she wanted was to hurry him to the gatehouse and nurse his wounds herself. He squeezed her fingers in return, the strength of his grip reassuring.

Remembering Miss Lyon's presence, Maryn let go of him only to find her rival running an appraising eye over her from tip to toe as if assessing her injury or in search of some sort of mourning jewelry.

If so, she looked in vain. Maryn loathed mourning jewelry. *Momento mori.* The fashionable Latin phrase that she would die one day was a lesson she'd learned well. She needn't wear black jewelry as a reminder.

"My deepest condolences, Your Grace," Miss Lyon said with a deep curtsey. "For the latest of many losses."

Maryn thanked her, silently wishing her on her way. Excusing himself, Orin went to fetch the coffee.

In his absence, Miss Lyon drew closer, her whisper sly. "I never thought to see a bereaved duchess in a bookshop."

"This duchess devours books," Maryn replied, forgetting her own infirmities completely in light of Orin's ambush.

The coffee finally appeared alongside Orin's explanation. "With Lisbon sugar and heavy cream."

"No dandelion coffee with pounded sugar candy?" she jested despite herself.

"A bonny memory though I've nae time for picking dandelions or pounding candy these days," he replied with a bruised smile.

"I should be serving you," she told him in concern.

She sat in the upholstered chair he offered near a window, her cup on the edge of a small table, Miss Lyon looking on. If she had interrupted a tête-à-tête she wasn't the least bit sorry. She wouldn't leave without settling the mystery of his coming to Lockhart Hall.

"Well, farewell for now, Mr. Hume," Miss Lyon said at last. "I suppose I shall see you at Lady Grainger's supper party this weekend?"

"My regrets," he replied easily. "Though I hope you enjoy it should you attend."

"But Lady Charis … " she said, clearly seeking answers.

"She's departed for England with the laird to attend a funeral."

"Ah, yes. Her suitor's father, the late duke. Pity, that."

No wedding for Charis then?

Saddened, Maryn took a sip of coffee, finding the exchange reserved. Far cooler than an almost betrothed couple would make. Had Nicola been right about their relationship? The question seemed moot when another woman appeared, clearly seeking the owner. Maryn watched the meeting play out in a sort of comic disbelief.

Was Wedderburn Books naught but a cover for courting?

Orin made introductions. "Miss Hazel Robson, Your Grace."

Dressed fashionably in violet silk and a bergère bonnet, she was English to the bone and so slender it seemed Maryn saw through her. To her credit, her demeanor was far more endearing than Miss Lyon's had been. But her winsome smile made Maryn increasingly uneasy.

She looked to her full cup, queasy. Whatever this terrible churning inside her portended, it was incompatible with strong coffee. Thoughts spinning along with her stomach, Maryn entertained an unwelcome possibility…

Had Miss Robson taken the place of Miss Lyon in his affections?

The lovely lass turned toward Orin in a sort of entreaty. "I've come to see how you're faring after such a terrible battering."

Orin made light of it though it seemed it pained him to even speak. "They might beat me but they'll nae defeat me."

"I commend you for your fortitude." She drew her lace shawl closer about her narrow shoulders. "I've also come to inquire about the book you ordered for me."

Orin summoned a clerk who quickly brought the tome in question. When the lad returned to dusting shelves, Miss Robson and Orin spoke quietly for a few moments, shopkeeper to customer. Or was there more?

"Good day, Your Grace," she said at last before Orin escorted her to the door. As Miss Robson departed with the book, Maryn felt little relief.

The door jingled shut and Orin returned to escort her into the privacy of his office. He took a seat behind his desk facing her while she took a chair. He looked at her mostly untouched cup. "Is the coffee not to your liking?"

She took a sip and looked at him tentatively, so heartsore she nearly couldn't speak. "The coffee is delicious but in truth I'm only thinking of you."

"I'll mend though I might have a scar or two." His expression mirrored concern for her. "I've nae seen you in Duns for some time."

She took a breath, wondering where to start. "I meant to come the very day you opened the bookshop but..."

His eyes clouded. "I'm sorry about your sister."

Sinking faster than the framed painting of a ship behind him, she wondered how to share all that had come to pass. His nearness—the events that had brought her here today—made her emotional. "I've been charged with raising my nieces and newborn nephew."

"The ones I saw you with when I last visited."

She nodded. "I'm sorry I missed you. Why did you go before I could speak with you?"

"You looked so happy with the bairns that I decided to leave the past alone."

"The past? What means you?"

He stood and went to a studded iron safe and unlocked it. When he returned he held letters tied with silk ribbon. Her letters... to him? Where had he found them? She took them, dazed. Yellowed with age, the ink faded, the seals had been broken.

"Marchmont stopped here before he left for France," he told her. "He found your letters among your sister's possessions after her death. I took them home to the gatehouse to read and then decided to keep them here."

"My letters... " Confusion muddled her. "Kept from you by Nicola?"

"It appears so."

All the girlish angst within those papers returned to her afresh. Even the flash of ire toward Nicola was buried beneath. She couldn't look at him so she pinned her gaze to the letters. "So, you... read them?"

"I did, aye. The seals were intact so I was the only one who did so."

She stared down at the outpourings of her heart. They needed to be fed to the fire. Her foolish regard of Orin Hume needed to die. At the very least she wanted to hurry home and stash the letters at the back of the desk in the secret compartment with his letters to her. As if she could contain her feelings inside that small space, stuff her heart into its confines and be done with it once and for all. But there was no denying she *still* felt the same about him—and always would.

"I've no words for all this," she murmured.

"Your letters said plenty."

Her heart caught at the feeling in his tone. She still couldn't meet his eyes, awash in what she'd written. "Perhaps Grandfather and Nicola conspired to keep us apart."

"Mayhap." He sat down again. "Suddenly it seems we're back where we left off five years ago. You've found my letters and I now have yours."

She forced herself to take another sip of the delicious coffee. When he reached toward the letters she staunched the urge to snatch them back. Instead, he retied the ribbon and returned them to the corner safe.

What did that signify?

"There's another matter." He pulled open a desk drawer and removed a book. "I found a rare tome in your collection I'd advise you keep. First published in 1609 and one of the original copies printed on English handmade paper."

A rare find, indeed. Thankful to change the subject, she took hold of the gilt-bound book. Shakespeare's sonnets? "*Let me not to the marriage of true minds...*" she began from memory.

He continued when her voice faltered. "*Love alters not with his brief hours and weeks, but bears it out even to the edge of doom...*"

"*If this be error and upon me proved; I never writ, nor no man ever loved,*" she finished.

They'd returned to their literary sparring of old. *Love alters not.* It reminded her of Scripture, the beloved verses in Corinthians. *Charity never faileth.*

The silence lengthened. She finished her coffee, the sonnets in her lap. When she looked up at him his attention was on the window fronting the busy street. She remembered the chaise. Rosemary would have had time enough for her ribbon.

"I must go," she said quietly. But she didn't want to leave.

Did he feel the same? That time was too fleeting? That so much remained unsaid that needed saying? Sometimes the heart held tight to all that defied words.

He saw her to the shop door then ushered her outside and helped her into the chaise where Rosemary waited. The withdrawal of his warm, strong hand left her utterly bereft.

28

Orin walked from the gatehouse to Wedderburn Castle in the gloaming. Was it only yesterday Maryn had left the bookshop? Mentally he'd retraced every exchanged word and look between them, including the fact, in a rare moment of angst, she'd called him *Orry*. Was she regretting that now?

He entered the castle's forecourt and was let in by a footman. The dining room wasn't far and the door was open as if he was expected. He walked toward it, remembering the laird and Charis would be away for some time given Yorkshire was so distant. Mayhap that was just as well. The countess was a keen listener and a wise counselor if he could unburden himself.

She turned away from the window when he entered, hands clasped in a sort of delight. "So I shan't dine alone after all."

"You might prefer it," he half-jested. "I'm poor company at present."

"Never that, though you do seem to be healing nicely." She smiled and they passed to the smaller chamber she preferred, the table set, a vase of crimson roses to one side, a few scattered petals on the damask cloth.

"The duchess sent the last of her heirloom summer roses round to me," Blythe said, admiring them. "She's kindly offered cuttings in hopes our gardeners can establish them here."

"I thought those had the look of Lockhart Hall." He took a seat, wondering if he could return there on the pretense of taking said cuttings. Nay. Gardener he was not.

"I'm afraid the menu may be too simple," Blythe said in apology once they'd said grace. "But in my advancing age rich dishes don't always agree with me."

"There's nothing wrong with brose and oatcakes."

"At least there's Crowdie cheese. You've been partial to that since you were a wee lad. And wild raspberry tarts."

He took an oatcake, trying to muster some appetite. Did Maryn dine alone or with the bairns?

"How goes the bookselling?" Blythe asked, touching on one of her favorite topics.

"Business is brisk. The reading room is now open. Yestreen I counted nearly twenty-six customers in the forenoon and half that many by closing. And nae more broken windows."

"Praise be." She sighed in relief. "The vandal was caught, I heard—and his penance is being taught to read."

"Aye. He's just a lad and helps out in the shop when he's not learning his letters from my clerks."

"A far more satisfying arrangement than the stocks. Bless you and your clerks."

"We're blessedly busy. Might you lend a hand?"

She laughed. "Everard would come after me if I did. He noted I spent half a day there last week but I simply couldn't help myself. Such a collection the duchess gave you!"

Maryn, again. He might as well confess she was his every waking thought. "She visited for the first time yesterday."

"Oh? And what did she think?"

"We never got around to that." All his carefully laid plans for showing her the shop folded once Miss Lyon and Miss Robson appeared. "Though I returned a rare copy of sonnets to her."

"Shakespeare, not Milton, I hope."

He chuckled. "Aye, the romantic rather than the tormented ones."

"So . . ." She looked up from spooning her soup. "Is there something you're not telling me?"

He hesitated. "There's something I'm not even telling myself."

"What means you?"

"I've only loved one lass my entire life and there won't be another."

"Does the lady in question know of your affection?"

"Other than giving her a hint by way of those sonnets? Nay."

"Then you should be on bended knee telling her, not me."

He smiled despite his discomfiture. "And if she doesn't want to hear it?"

"What woman in her right mind would refuse you?" She nearly glared at him. "You're the best of all possible worlds. Courtier. Poet. Playwright. Bookseller . . ."

"I finally approached her not long ago as a matter of honor, testing our former tie." He looked to the roses again, the memory still sore. "She said there's nae going back to what was. That we're different people now."

"And yet she came to visit you at the bookshop yesterday."

"As friends, aye."

"Given she's recently become a mother to four children, including the future heir to the duchy should she have none, I would guess she's having second thoughts about raising them without a fatherly influence. Lord Marchmont is not long for this world, I fear. His lung ailment is quite advanced. He may not return from France, sadly."

He'd heard the man was very ill. Losing one's wife didn't help either. "Do you also ken that Nicola and the late duke seem to have conspired to prevent Maryn's and my relationship from continuing by confiscating the letters we wrote to each other after the accident?"

"I did not." Blythe put a serviette to her lips. "I condemn that sort of scheming interference though it isn't my place to judge."

"Letters aside, I canna continue to pursue her if she's unwilling."

"As a matter of honor, nay." Blythe buttered an oat cake and eyed his mostly untouched meal. "But you can continue to pray about it. I've certainly not stopped. In fact, my petitions on that heartfelt subject have increased of late."

As had his. Did his deep appreciation show? He picked up his spoon, knowing he needed to eat.

"Though I've heard, from well-placed sources, that there are other ladies who are vying for your attention at present."

"Your daughter is trying her best to play matchmaker, aye." With Charis away, *that* he didn't miss.

"Since you feel the way you do about Maryn, I don't suppose you've given serious thought to anyone else."

He'd tried to set aside his hopes and desires to weigh that very matter in a more practical light. Miss Lyon was not someone he'd forge a future with but Miss Robson? She was kind, courteous, well read and more. But his half-heartedness regarding her, in light of his passion for Maryn, seemed pale, indeed. A lass deserved better than a lackluster suitor and husband.

He took a drink of Madeira. "Do you believe there are more sorts of love than one? That you can let go of what you hoped for and settle for someone and something else?"

"There are all sorts of love, yes. But there's only one shining kind on which to build a marriage. A life."

They finished the remainder of their meal deep in thought. Coffee was served, again reminding him of Maryn. He missed her with a physical ache. Was there no relief for this longing to be with her? To sit down with her for meals. To walk with her in the garden. To hold her at night. To discuss books and mayhap even pen plays together. Even becoming the proxy father of four overnight increased his yearning.

Was he mad?

"I believe I shall walk with you to the gatehouse," Blythe said as they rose from the table. "The lovely evening begs to be admired."

Together they left the castle's forecourt to watch the sunset overlay the landscape in a rainbow of hues. The gloaming's hush eased his turmoil somewhat.

"You miss the laird, I sense," he said, his steadying hand on her elbow. "And Charis."

"It seems a long separation at an unfortunate time. But death is never timely."

"I recall when Everard rode to England and petitioned the king on your behalf years ago."

"So long ago! I feared I'd never see either of you again. But here we are. Life has a way of exceeding our expectations. The Lord, rather."

"You've been happy here in the Lowlands though you're an Englishwoman."

"Ours has been a bountiful life despite its challenges. And did I tell you? Once Everard and Charis return we're to have a family gathering. All your brothers and their families will be here—and all our sons, Lord willing."

"So, my nephews are returning from the Grand Tour in time?" At her nod, he asked, "Will the castle hold them all?"

"We shall see." She smiled, her pleasure plain, as well as her pathos when she looked at him. "I want that same happiness for you, Orin. The joy of family. A home. Of coming together with the lady you love."

He looked heavenward, an unspoken prayer rising.

As do I.

29

This was, by far, the hardest thing she'd ever done. The quill in Maryn's hand fluttered like the birds in Orin's poem she'd committed to memory. Yet despite her nerves, it felt right. She held on to her courage when her nieces stormed her cabinet as if discovering a secret hideaway, their high-pitched voices a welcome distraction.

Charlotte began playing with the miniature bust of Romeo and Juliet sitting at the desk's edge. "Aunt Maryn, what do you do in here when you're not with us?"

Pray. Write. Ponder. Dream.

Maryn set down her quill. "Well, your great-grandfather left me plenty to do when he went to heaven and so I try to be a good steward of all that God gave us."

"Mama said baby Haddon will be a duke one day." Penelope asked, "Is that true?"

"Perhaps." Maryn smiled. Nicola's vision reached beyond the grave, truly. "But that is a long ways off and much can happen between now and then."

"I should like to be a duchess like you," Charlotte continued, her pale curls framing her dimpled face. "And I would like to wear a tiara. Do you have a tiara?"

"Yes, more than one. Recently I found jewelry in your late grandmother's dressing room. Would you like to see all of that after tea today? We can play dress-up."

They giggled in delight and Pen said, "We shall pretend to be princesses."

Smelling of the lavender sewn into the hem of her gown, Eugenie climbed into Maryn's lap. Bareheaded, she was missing her cap again but Maryn didn't have the heart to scold her. She didn't like wearing hers either. Seizing the quill, Eugenie started dabbing the inked tip onto the letter Maryn had abandoned, making her second guess her decision to write it.

Soon Nurse appeared in the midst of the melee, chuckling at the sight of all three gathered round the large desk. "Mercy, Yer Grace, ye have a saint's patience!"

The girls rushed to her, telling her about playing dress-up as Eugenie climbed down from Maryn's lap. In moments, Nurse shooed them from the room, leaving stillness in their wake. And an ink-splattered letter. With a sigh, Maryn began anew, taking out a fresh sheet of foolscap.

Did she have the heart to continue?

Lord, help.

She wished she had some lighthearted verse in mind but this was no lighthearted matter.

Inking her quill again, she began.

Thursday, 27 September...

When autumn set in, Wedderburn's Books became even busier. October brought russet red to the moors, the Scots pines holding tight to their green amid the scarlet-golds of the maples and oaks. A land of mist and melancholy, Orin thought as he rode into Duns at the start of another day.

Another day he'd likely not see Maryn. The twenty-sixth day, exactly. He'd fought an ongoing battle, reining himself in when he felt he couldn't go another minute without her, a longing that only seemed to intensify instead of abate. Caught in the crux of the matter, he'd become a man of prayer instead of pining away like the lovesick would-be suitor he disdained.

Maryn's absence spoke volumes. She had, it seemed, moved on with her new family and a far fuller life than anyone would ever have imagined. The babe he'd not yet seen would be getting bigger by the day. He didn't ken much about infants but he knew Maryn would make a fine mother even if the children weren't her own.

"Promise you'll come for supper," Charis had told him last night when he'd joined them after a sennight's absence. "You are spending too much time alone when not in that bookshop of yours."

He thought of it now as he stabled his horse then walked down the lane that led to the bookshop. In truth, he hadn't much appetite for food or conversation of late. The gatehouse was lonely at times, aye, but he'd come round to a routine. Working late. Having a simple supper alone. Evenings found him reading by the hearth. He'd given up penning poetry or plays altogether. There seemed little romance left in his soul.

"Good morn, sir," one of his shop clerks said behind him. "A wee bite in the wind, aye?"

"More than a bite," Orin replied, unlocking the door with a clank of keys. "The laird predicts an early frost and an exceedingly cold winter."

"Och, my da says the verra same." He grimaced as he removed his hat and hung it from a peg. "His auld bones are like a weathervane."

"Reminds me of the Thames freezing over, all the way up to London Bridge." Orin rarely thought of his former life other than his London colleagues. "Even the ink in the inkwells froze. *That* I do not miss."

He took up Maryn's coffee-mill to grind a fresh batch at the hearth. It cast him back to the day she'd sat with him in his office. What pleasure he'd taken serving her and having her to himself for even a half hour.

Would that be his last memory of her?

He looked out the nearest window. With the wind keening around the shop's corners and scattering brittle leaves, autumn seemed especially bittersweet. Change swept him along likewise, reminding him of the passage of time as assuredly as the calendar on his desk.

Perhaps today Maryn would return to Duns. A thousand times he'd imagined their reunion. Perhaps she'd bring the bairns. He'd began a search for children's books but found few except for fairytales and fables. He'd even begun reading John Locke's volume on child-rearing. Framed in his head and heart was a picture of Maryn and her nieces playing on the lawn at Lockhart Hall, their laughter still ringing inside him.

Though he wanted more from her, he was willing to take her friendship if that was all she could offer. Yet such would cost him dearly. It meant the death of his desires. His long-held hopes and plans. But so be it. In the end, he was just a simple man of honor who relied on heaven itself to change her mind.

To restore the years the locusts had eaten.

30

As November swept in on a strong easterly gale, Maryn continued her mothering, resigning herself to staying indoors. October had been among the coldest on record, the newspapers predicting a harsh winter. Even the servants were discussing it as they gathered in extra coal and firewood. Weather, however, was the farthest thing from her mind.

Was Orin well and safe? Who knew that opening a bookstore could be dangerous? Surely she would have heard any ill tidings regarding him. Lowland news spread like midges. Though the door between them had shut, a window to her soul remained open. She kept him close in spirit, ever praying for his protection and blessing.

As daylight grew shorter other concerns beset her. Had she been wrong to seek refuge in writing him a letter instead of speaking to him in person? She'd always been better on paper. Professing one's true feelings was best done in print, surely, at least where she was concerned.

As the days passed with no reply from him, she felt cut to the quick with other questions. Was she a coward for waiting till he left for the bookshop that September day before leaving her letter in the gatehouse's garden wall? Might he have forgotten all about the way they secreted letters there in the past? Mightn't wind and weather have snatched the sealed paper away?

Or perhaps he had found it and already read it. Dismissed it out of hand. Perhaps her phrasing put him off and he'd decided to pursue the bonny Englishwoman after all. She didn't blame him. Who wouldn't want a fresh start without the weight of a complicated past?

Mercy, she'd gone gyte, half mad with longing and wondering.

Each day she waited, hoping for his answer. An answer she anticipated with nearly every breath. The only post she'd received other than her literary contacts was from Lord Marchmont saying he hoped spring would have him turn a corner to better health. She wrote back, telling him in lavish detail all that his daughters were saying and doing and the extraordinary growth of his son. Even Nurse said she'd never seen so thriving a lad which relieved Maryn immensely.

Meanwhile, she was reveling in being their second mother. Who knew that tantrums increased when bellies were empty? Or that a nap often resulted in sunny smiles all around? Fresh air and sunshine did wonders, too. As for Charlotte, she'd managed to procure a governess, a gently born woman who would arrive in spring. Her plans for her nieces' and nephew's welfare were unending.

But first the coming winter needed managing. Aside from estate matters which Hutchins was assuming with aplomb, she now had time for more pleasant pursuits like her tambour embroidery, having a standing frame built to better accommodate her injury.

"Yer Grace, the babe's napped and been fed and is ready for ye." Nurse appeared at the doorway of the morning room, Haddon somewhat swaddled. His plump arms snuck free of the linen as he waved his wee fists about.

"I'll gladly take him and walk about the Portrait Gallery since the weather is less than clement. Meanwhile, Cook has prepared a delightful tea for you and Fiona." Maryn smiled at her, grateful for both nurses. "Don't give the babe and I another thought."

Until he bellows, she refrained from saying.

She felt at sixes and sevens when he cried for no apparent reason. Was he hungry again? Did he need changing? Or was a misplaced pin sticking him? Perhaps his skin was irritated and in need of powdering. She looked forward to the day when he could tell her the trouble himself.

Once again she grew pensive. How would Orin manage him? She could see him so clearly, handling Haddon as a loving father would do. Or had the prospect of being a second parent pushed him away?

Awed, she took her near-perfect nephew in one arm. Soon she'd not be able to hold him as he'd grow too big. Recently she'd read that the Duke of Devonshire had commissioned a landscape architect to fashion a fancy wheeled contraption to carry his children about. Perhaps a less elaborate, wicker one could be crafted to hold Haddon.

She walked the length of the immense chamber, the walls lined with all the Fordyces of centuries past. As she pondered their legacy she considered her own. Grandfather's will had specified that as duchess a portrait be painted of her soon after his passing. Perhaps a family portrait would be best. Children, if they could stand still long enough, would be a beautiful study for an artist's brush.

If nothing else, they would be her legacy. She might never marry or have children of her own but she could raise her sister's, Lord willing, and see that they became strong, stalwart adults with no memory of the Lockhart curse.

'Twas snowing. On the very date of the tragedy that took Herschel and removed Maryn from his life. As a lad, he'd rejoiced in the snow which transformed the bleak winter landscape into a sort of fairy kingdom. And then the accident happened, stealing the magic. The whistle of the December wind around the eaves added another layer of melancholy as the Sabbath ebbed.

Orin added seasoned pine to the hearth's fire since the gatehouse's chimney hadn't been refitted for coal like the rest of Wedderburn Castle. But he liked the old ways best. The snap and tang of a wood fire was something he'd miss. Mayhap he needed a dog to keep him company. Something other than the stray cat he'd been feeding. Nothing like a creaturely companion if a lass was lacking. Done with his simple supper of bread and cheese and an orchard apple, he bypassed his bookshelves to take in the storm.

Standing by the parlor window overlooking the gatehouse garden, he tried to make peace with the passage of time and summon some of that wintry magic. Snow brought a hallowed, ethereal hush to the landscape. The garden's stone wall was muted now, its slate-grey icy white. Wedderburn Castle sat in back of it a mile distant, a blur of wind and weather.

The flash of a chaffinch's wings caught his eye. The rust-breasted creature gave him pause. It alighted on the stone ledge of the garden wall right above the crevice meant for letters and began what looked to be a courtship dance. The whimsical spectacle ended but the wee bird stayed where it was, drawing attention to something else entirely.

Orin blinked. Leaned into the frozen windowpane. What was that bit of blue beneath? His imagination?

The chaffinch began to sing, a melodic burst of trills and chirps. Odd, that, on such a day. But odder still was the spot of blue. With no thought to his hat or coat, Orin strode out the back door into the whirl of white. Upon sight of him the bird took wing as if its work was done.

Across the frozen garden he trod in sark, breeches, and boots, intent on the wall. His heart began to sprint as if he'd run all the way to the castle instead. Carefully, his fingers felt the icy opening. A paper? Aye. Sealed with blue wax. Maryn's seal. Freed of its confines, the once fine foolscap was wet and fragile in his cold hand.

A burst of wind pushed against him, sending snow from the ledge into his face. Turning away, he hastened back inside, gripping the paper lest it fly away like the chaffinch.

Slamming shut the door, he made his way to the hearth where light fell upon the wax seal as he broke it. Dismay pummeled him. Within the letter itself, the ink had bled and run, all but a few words. Blast! The exact date was missing—September? He groaned aloud. More than two months ago. A few *ands* and *buts* he recognized but the rest of the handwriting was an untidy mess. All but the last words at the very bottom...

Ever thine, Maryn

Thunderstruck, he was. His heart was a-gallop now. He tried to make out more faded sentences. Failed. To Hades with the rest.

Those final three words were the only ones that mattered.

31

The first snow of the season seemed a gift and the children's joy doubled Maryn's. Dressed warmly in thick wool capes and boots and mittens, she led her nieces outside to whirl about like snowflakes and make snow angels. Nessie raced around in delirious circles, further amusing them. As the icy mantle climbed to Maryn's shins, she looked out over the whitewashed Lowlands, wishing she could share it with someone not so wee.

"Auntie, can we eat the snow?" Pen asked, catching snowflakes on her tongue.

"Of course, Poppet," Maryn said, doing the same. "When I was wee, we used to mix snow with sugar. Snow cream, we called it. Your mother loved it like I did."

"Let's make some!" Charlotte jumped up and down, her cheeks pink as the wintering roses in the glasshouse behind her.

"I'll fetch a dish, then." Maryn started toward a near door, first rescuing Eugenie who'd fallen into a snow drift. Dusting her off, she watched as her youngest niece returned to play with her sisters.

Once inside, Maryn nearly ran into Mrs. Duncan. "Your Grace, you've a visitor."

A visitor? Had she misheard?

Maryn pushed three words past frozen lips. "In this weather?"

The housekeeper's smile seemed to light up the hall. "Aye, and only the most stalwart, brawest Scots will brave it. In this case, Mr. Hume." Mrs. Duncan gestured toward an open door. "In your cabinet."

Suddenly breathless, Maryn remembered her nieces. "Please have someone watch over the children outside. I promised them snow cream. And bring a buttered toddy for Mr. Hume."

"Of course. Now, let me help you with your wraps." She took Maryn's damp cape then left her alone in the hall to collect herself.

Why had Orin come? And on the Sabbath, to boot. Did he remember it was the anniversary of Herschel's death? Looking down at her soaked hem, she discarded the notion of rushing to her bedchamber to make herself presentable. Concern—and yearning—forbade any delay. She approached the chamber dearest her heart, amazed the man who held her heart waited there.

He faced the hearth's leaping fire, his back to the door as she entered. He'd shed his coat and hat but his hair, caught back with black ribbon, was damp. She framed his sturdy shoulders and remarkable height in her mind's eye as joy filled her to the brim, so overwhelmingly she felt faint.

"Orry..." she finally said as he turned toward her. His features were ruddy with cold. The light and joy in his face struck her hard as the snow. Only a slight, telltale scar remained beneath his injured eye.

"Maryn."

For a moment they just stood, their gazes locked, and then he took something from his pocket.

"A wee bird—a chaffinch—lit on the garden wall right above this. I'd given up checking the opening last summer. And then today..."

Her September letter? Had he finally found it? Warmth suffused her cheeks as she remembered all she'd penned.

"The weather erased all but a few words." He held it out to her. "Dismayed as I was to find it so long after you'd written it, the fact that it was there gave me hope."

She took the ink-smeared paper from him, now so weathered and worn. Perhaps the tenderest things needed to be spoken, after all.

"I wrote that I've decided to *live* life rather than lock myself away from it. A life that includes you." She paused, a bit winded by so many heartfelt words, unable to raise her gaze as she laid bare her heart. "Unless I read you wrongly, you seem to want me by your side, not only as a matter of honor."

"Maryn, look at me." His fingers brushed her cheek, startling cold against her flushed skin. "Sometimes it's even hard for a poet to express how he feels. I phrased it as a matter of honor but that includes my enduring love. A love that will not fade or find satisfaction in someone else."

He took her wounded hand and held it in his for a few seconds before gently removing her glove. Unable to look at her scarred, stitched-together flesh, she searched his face but his expression showed only compassion.

"I've said it before but it bears repeating. I would give all that I am to undo that day."

"As would I." She swallowed, summoning details she'd uttered to no one. "There's something you should ken before we go further. The doctors who treated me after the accident said my injuries aren't just the ones that can be seen. If we were to—" she faltered, out of her depth, "—come together, I may be unable to conceive..."

A flash of amusement crossed his face. "Four bairns are nae enough?" He brought her fingers to his lips. "Will you have me, then, come what may?"

Would she? "I will have you without any further delay. And I shan't be wearing sable."

"Then I'll do what the laird did when he wed his Northumberland bride. I'll forego the banns and obtain a special license."

"We'll wed at Ladykirk if you like." The wonder of it nearly stole speech. "With three flower girls attending us."

His gaze lifted as howls erupted from upstairs. "And one rowdy lad whom I've yet to meet."

No sooner had he said it than Haddon quieted.

He turned serious. "My lack of title is of nae consequence to you? Nor any naysayers?"

"I've never cared about either." She looked toward the cabinet's windows. Snow continued to sift down like sugar, overlaying the land like the richest icing on a wedding cake. "At the moment I feel far more a bride than a duchess. And you might well be snowed in here till we marry."

"There's nae place I'd rather be."

She turned back to him, their hands clasped, wanting no secrets between them. "I have another confession. I'm a playwright. A poet. But not of your caliber or stature."

"Only because there's nae Poet Laureate lass of Britain yet." His regard told her he wasn't surprised. "I suspected you'd never stopped your literary endeavors, including founding a renowned gazette. Something about queens and bees..."

Her smile was bittersweet. "I sought refuge in my writing when life was at its darkest."

"Nae more dark days, Maryn, at least alone." His voice deepened with emotion. "In future we'll weather them together."

He leaned in, the touch of his lips like a caress. Her arm encircled his neck, bringing him nearer, so close she felt the pulse of his heart beneath his linen sark, her rose-scented softness enveloped in his embrace.

He kissed her again and again, moving from her lips to her throat, the hollow of her shoulder, her hands, leaving a trail of tingling fire. His low murmur against her hair left her equally undone. "Mrs. Hume *née* the Duchess of Fordyce, then."

"Forever and ever, amen."

Author's Postscript

This Scottish tale was inspired by my love of birds, books, and blooms. I owe that to my precious mom, Irene Sylvia Blanton, whose wonder of the natural world & the written word never fades. I'm only now fully realizing the rich legacy she gave me as she nears ninety years of age.

If you've read my full-length historical romance novel, *The Rose and the Thistle,* you might remember Orin Hume being the youngest of the clan. It was wonderful to grow him up & give him his own love story in this companion novella. For more of my Hume ancestry/history, please refer to the author note in *The Rose and the Thistle.*

As for this story, the periodical *Tatler* was in print only briefly at the beginning of the 18th-century but I continued to circulate it within these pages. I've also included a number of references to poetry and literary works popular at the time and now in the public domain. The lovely line, "I retain an unalterable affection for you, which neither time or distance can change" is from a letter George Washington wrote to Martha Washington in 1775. The bird poem was by a tenth century Irish poet.

Heartfelt thanks to Hannah Linder for capturing the romantic gist of this novella & my design hopes. That gown & gatehouse! Kudos to Grace Johnson for providing a stellar critique that lent this story wings. Endless thanks to Shelli Littleton for proofreading the manuscript more than once. Your eagle eye & love for edifying fiction is truly a gift. Heartfelt thanks to Mary Kay Moody. Your perusal of the finished novella helped me revise a critical scene. Your help was heavensent.

God never gives or gifts us a story then leaves us alone to finish it. I felt His Presence on every page, even in so simple a novella as this, & hope it has merit and meaning to someone else.

About the Author

Laura Frantz is a two time Christy Award winner and the ECPA bestselling author of sixteen novels, including *An Uncommon Woman, Tidewater Bride, A Bound Heart, A Heart Adrift, The Rose and the Thistle,* and *The Seamstress of Acadie.* She is the proud mom of an American soldier and a career firefighter. Though Kentucky will always be home to her, she and her husband live in Washington State. Learn more at LauraFrantz.net.

Books by Laura Frantz

The Frontiersman's Daughter
Courting Morrow Little
The Colonel's Lady
The Mistress of Tall Acre
A Moonbow Night
The Lacemaker
A Bound Heart
An Uncommon Woman
Tidewater Bride
A Heart Adrift
The Rose and the Thistle
The Seamstress of Acadie
The Indigo Heiress

THE BALLANTYNE LEGACY
Love's Reckoning
Love's Awakening
Love's Fortune

Made in the USA
Middletown, DE
20 July 2024

57674669R00124